PENGUIN
A HIMALAYAN L

Namita Gokhale was born in Luckand grew up in Nainital and New Delhi. She began her career publishing a popular film magazine, *Super*. Her first novel, *Paro: Dreams of Passion*, was published in 1984, followed by *Gods, Graves and Grandmother* (1994), *Mountain Echoes* (1997), *The Book of Shadows* (1999) and *The Book of Shiva* (2001).

Namita Gokhale lives in New Delhi with her two daughters.

saraswathi editions
Cochin, India

A HIMALAYAN LOVE STORY

NAMITA GOKHALE

PENGUIN BOOKS

Penguin Books India (P) Ltd., 11 Community Centre, Panchsheel Park, New Delhi 110 017, India
Penguin Books Ltd., 80 Strand, London WC2R 0RL, UK
Penguin Putnam Inc., 375 Hudson Street, New York, NY 10014, USA
Penguin Books Australia Ltd., 250 Camberwell Road, Camberwell, Victoria 3124, Australia
Penguin Books Canada Ltd., 10 Alcorn Avenue, Suite 300, Toronto, Ontario M4V 3B2, Canada
Penguin Books (NZ) Ltd., Cnr Rosedale & Airborne Roads, Albany, Auckland, New Zealand

First published by Har-Anand Publications 1996
This revised edition published by Penguin Books India 2002

Typeset in Sabon by Mantra Virtual Services, New Delhi
Printed at Chaman Offset Printers, New Delhi

CONTENTS

CONTENTS

PARVATI:
THE DANCE OF THE HONEYBEE

I have always recognized that I carry an emptiness inside me, although I did not at first understand it. When I was a child, I would look at other faces, at their ordinary expressions of laughter and sadness and tears, and wonder at the ease with which they juggled these masks about. All I ever felt was a constant festering sense of anger and unease. I felt trapped inside my skin and bone and circumstance, and for this reason I began at a very early age to avoid people.

I grew up in Jeolikote, a popular tourist halt on the road to Nainital. The two rooms my mother and I occupied were perched above a small kirana shop and belonged to my mother's brother, who was the headmaster of a public school in Nainital. They were connected by a small veranda, and overlooked the highway. Every summer the smell of diesel would assail our senses, and the incessant hooting and parping of the tourist buses would keep us awake. Otherwise the surroundings were sylvan, even idyllic. Rhododendrons, the local 'Burush', covered the slopes in March, and in April sharp red flowers illuminated the Krishnakali trees. A whole host of short-lived flowers bloomed and died through the rest of the year: arum lilies, gladioli, tiger lilies, marigolds, poinsettias, and the holly and mistletoe that grew in December and were sent to shops in Delhi for Christmas. If you took the path that wound behind the house up to the top of the hill, you would find the small sour strawberries, for which Jeolikote was famous, growing in splendid abundance. These were sold in cane baskets to the summer tourists, cunningly disguised in weight and worth by the heap of mulberry leaves on which they were artfully spread out.

Strawberries, mulberries and roasted corn on the cob were the staples of trade in Jeolikote, apart, of course, from the honey for which it was justly famous. It was not a prosperous town, nor a particularly interesting one. Subjects of conversation were few and far between; nothing much happened except for yet another tourist or traveller taking sick because of the winding roads and puking uninhibitedly out of the window onto the body of a bus. Once, when I was seven, a rabid dog had terrorized our town for all of two months; my mother and I felt thankful for our safe perch on the upper storey of the kirana shop, and briefly we felt lucky, superior in fate to those unfortunates who lived in sprawling bungalows and were therefore completely at the mercy of the mad marauder. And one winter in the 1940s it was reported that there was a man-eating tiger on the prowl. I can never forget the stark terror that possessed us when we had to perforce use the open-air privy behind our house. My mother would stand guard holding a burning branch of cactus bush in her hand, and then, after I was through, I would hold guard for her. A permanent knot of tension developed in my stomach, and I refused to go to school or run any errands for my mother. Jim Corbett, already a folk hero in the hills, had left his adoptive home by then and settled in Africa. The locals bewailed his absence and lived in terror till an intrepid forest ranger shot the tiger point-blank and killed it.

Apart from occasions like these, life in Jeolikote was dull, and the principal conversation of the town in such epochs of peace was bee-keeping. There was nobody in Jeolikote who was not knowledgeable about bee-keeping, it had entered our very souls by some process of osmosis. The local government had established The Model Bee-keeping Institute with a view to providing alternative employment for our hill folk, who had until then fled with unfailing regularity to the plains for recruitment into the army or employment as domestic servants or cooks in the households of northern India. This money-order economy quite literally revolved around the post office, and the postmaster sahib was the hub of social and economic life.

We had nobody who sent money orders to us. My father had died of tuberculosis when I was a year old. I had no brothers and sisters. Our only living relative was my mother's stepbrother, Hiranand Joshi, who was, as I have mentioned, the principal of a school—the Manava Public School—in Nainital. He was a mean and humourless man whom we both hated. He despised us in return, but he had given us no actual cause for our hatred, and was indeed unfailing in the execution of his duties, having provided us with the house in which we lived, besides allowing us to collect rent from the kirana shop for our sustenance.

It was not clear why he despised us so, but I suspected some ancient and unequal childhood rivalry. My mother had, I believe, been a beautiful and spirited girl, and even now, years of poverty and deprivation had not managed to breach her pride. She could tongue-lash anybody in Jeolikote who trod on her sensibilities, and her eyes were frequently aflash with anger as she confronted yet another dupe who had mistakenly dealt with her as a vulnerable widow.

My mother was completely illiterate. She had been married at the age of thirteen to the second son of a well-to-do family of Almora, who had quickly spent his entire fortune on gambling and other addictions. When at the age of thirty-two he was afflicted with tuberculosis, there was simply no money for his treatment. Mercifully, he had died without much ado, and my mother's stepbrother, my uncle Hiranand Joshi, had gallantly come to her aid and bought the kirana shop as an investment. He was always on the lookout for properties which he could buy cheaply through bankruptcies, distress sales and the like. 'Masterji', as he was known in Jeolikote, was an important man in Nainital, and my mother was constantly importuned with letters of reference for admission to his school and requests for waiver of fees and suchlike, all of which she gracefully accepted but never showed him. Masterji had thus achieved a quite undeserved reputation in Jeolikote for being 'unhelpful', still the hopeful letters and introductions did not cease.

My uncle had insisted that I be given an education, and in view of her circumstances my mother had no option but to accede to his wishes. Nevertheless she considered it a waste of money. She would complain bitterly about the cost of books and uniforms, although the actual school fees were of course heavily subsidized. 'It would be different if you were a boy,' she would say angrily, 'then you could earn and provide for me in my old age. But all you are going to do is get married to some no-good, and take my gold champakali necklace off with you as dowry. It's a double curse, to first be born a woman, then get straddled with another female to provide for!'

Of course she did not really have to provide for me, for the rent from the shop adequately covered our meagre requirements. We had an absolute minimum of needs: two sets of clothing each, three warm sweaters between the two of us, and one and a half meals a day. In the mid-morning we ate a meal of watery dal and rice. In the evenings, invariably, we ate potatoes. There were a hundred ways in which my mother knew how to cook potatoes—aloo ke gutke, aloo ka pani, aloo tomato, aloo matar and so on. We had the potatoes with the leftover rice from the mornings, and sometimes mother would make chapattis.

There was a chai-wala in the market to whom my grandfather, my father's father, had once in better days lent some money. Every morning, unfailingly, he sent us a brass tumblerful of cow's milk, warm and frothing, from which my mother carefully extracted the cream, and so we had enough ghee to smear on the thick chapattis she reluctantly cooked.

I suppose that by the standards of those times we were not badly off. We had a pucca house to live in. We had no electricity but enough kerosene oil most days to light a couple of bottle lamps, even a lantern. And we had a bricked-up choolha which had to be daily smeared with cowdung. Lighting the choolha was a strenuous enterprise, involving much huffing and blowing through a metal nali, so that our kitchen was always smoky, and the dal, the milk, the rotis, all had an acrid taste of smoke.

It was my job to gather the firewood. Every day, after I returned from school, I would deposit my slate and school books under the bed, and set out to look for kindling. The lower branches of mulberry trees and young bushes and lichen-encrusted twigs were all easily accessible, but they burnt badly; they did not light easily, and when they did they crackled and smoked and became ash all at once. My mother chided me about this, and urged me to look for dryer, older wood, but I was too timid to clamber up the oak and sal trees as the other children did. Of course my mother could have gone and gathered the wood herself, but she was far too proud for this: after all, she was a Brahmin, not a ghasyaran, and her stepbrother was an educated man, the principal of the Manava Public School in Nainital!

Every autumn we would sit down together in the yard behind the house and mix a messy concoction of cow dung and mud, which we then made into round pats. It was my job to arrange these dung cakes in neat rows on the sloping tin roof of our house, where they could dry in the bright October sun. As I clambered on to the roof I was always awkward and afraid, certain that I would fall off and land in a heap on the pavement in front of the shop. Afterwards there was still the ordeal of retrieving them, bringing them down in baskets, braving the vertigo as I faced the void below and crept cautiously down the rickety ladder my mother borrowed from the kirana shop for such expeditions.

It was our ambition to buy a cow. Everybody of any substance in Jeolikote owned a cow. The more prosperous families had procured Jersey cows from the veterinary centre at Mukteswar, while the rest made do with the more humble native Pahari breeds. My mother thought up many schemes to raise the money, none of which ever worked. We cleared a patch of land behind the shop, and raised a splendid harvest of corn. But there was a surfeit of corn that year, and after my mother had subcontracted with the chai-wala, disaster struck. The chai-wala decamped to Kathgodam on a drunken binge, where he fell off the railway platform onto the tracks and was mashed to pulp by an incoming train from

Lucknow. Since his wife was not as generous as he had been, even our supplies of free milk dried up. Moreover, we were stuck with vast quantities of corn which we didn't know how to dispose of. We had to eat corn every day, and still there was plenty left over, which my mother hung from the kitchen rafters for the winter months. I began to hate the taste of corn, and the grains stuck between my teeth and had to be extracted with the help of a hard green pine needle, which I used as a toothpick.

My mother was famous for her knitting, she could copy any pattern she saw and she had a neat, firm hand. A rich lady whose daughter studied with me commissioned my mother to knit several sweaters, the wool and patterns for which she obtained all the way from Bareilly. I can still remember the feel of the soft angora and lambswool. Mother got down to work, and, before my eyes, kittens cavorted across front-open cardigans and winsome bunnies emerged from the skeins of wool. Soon five hand-knitted sweaters lay in a neat pile on my mother's bed.

'Let me keep one of them,' I begged, 'just one!' But Mother was adamant; we couldn't afford it. 'Then let me try them on,' I said, 'just to see how they feel.' The request was indignantly turned down, although she did soften, and promised to knit me a tasselled scarf after the Sahji's wife had paid her.

We went together to deliver the sweaters. Before we reached the bungalow I pressed the soft angora creation against my cheek. Lata Sah, the girl in my class for whom they were intended, met us at the gate. She glanced casually at the sweaters, but betrayed none of the excitement and happiness I would have expected. Inside, I watched as my mother humbly laid out her handiwork on the lacy tablecloth. Lata's mother wore a topaz ring, and on her crowded wrists heavy gold bracelets clanked musically against green glass bangles. She examined my mother's offerings with a critical eye, stretching and pulling them to see if the stitches were taut enough. Lata was instructed to try them on. She pirouetted around the room and modelled them for us. Mother tried hard to look unconcerned and business-like, but when Mrs Sah finally nodded her approval and reached into her full bosom for the money, her face broke into a relieved smile. After she had counted the notes, Mother handed over the balls of leftover wool to Lata's mother, and we returned home.

We still did not have enough money to buy a cow but Mother was optimistic. There were always ways and means to earn a little extra money. The postmaster suggested that Mother take to bee-keeping. He was full of newfangled ideas like that: his son lived in Bombay and his daughter was studying to become a teacher. Mother liked the idea. 'There's something to it,' she agreed. We got the pamphlets from the bee-keeping institute, and she made me read them out to her. 'Perhaps Masterji is right, Parvati,' she said. 'Your education might turn out to be of some use after all. Look at the postmaster's daughter, she'll get into service soon. You could become a teacher!' I imagined myself confronting a class full of children; I knew I could never do it. I turned back to the pamphlet, and tried to explain the economics of bee-keeping to her.

Bees interested me, particularly the segregation of the sexes and the clear demarcation of their roles. I could make sense of it and relate it to my surroundings. Our Pahari men were always crowding around the local tea shops, playing cards or purposefully spitting out tobacco. They were the drones who gratefully left the labour to their women, the thin, hardy ghasyarans who balanced incredible heights of fodder and fuelwood on their heads. Personages like Lata Sah's mother, with her gold and glass bangles and her appetite for leftover balls of wool, were the queen bees.

I often read the *Introduction to Bee-keeping* out loud to myself. 'Male bees are usually short-lived,' I would intone, my customary shyness with English quite forgotten. 'They never collect pollen, nor have they any other responsibilities in connection with providing for their young. Female bees do all the work of nest-making and provisioning.' I read about solitary bees and social bees, and of the dance of the honeybee as it senses and searches for pollen. My knowledge was destined to remain theoretical, for we never got down to actual bee-keeping. One day, as my mother was sitting in the veranda, watching the buses from Rampur and Delhi come in, a bee stung her. She ran in screaming, and told me to get some limestone from the kirana shop, which I smeared over her swollen cheek. It became infected and gave her trouble for a long time. She decided she had no luck with bees, and we abandoned the idea. We never made the extra money to afford a cow.

*

The kirana shop below our house, which sold all manner of groceries, was rented out to a man from Haldwani. He was a silent, watchful sort of man who sat quietly amidst the heaps and mounds of rice and lentils and gunny bags full of sugar and foodgrains, lazily staring out at the blue haze on the hills across the road. Masterji had slipped up in his analysis, for Jeolikote talk held this man to be slightly disreputable. Mother maintained an account with him, which she was often forgetful about. Shrikrishnji, however, was extremely punctual and scrupulous about the rent, and never adjusted it against our borrowings—as well he could have. It was rumoured that he drank, but we had no evidence for it, for he always remained seated silently in his shop staring at nothing in particular.

That winter our funds were running very low. It was colder than ever and we had to resort to buying coal and firewood from the market. I wore my black woollen cardigan and mother her red one, and we huddled next to each other at night, but it was no use. Our teeth would chatter in the cold, and we would console each other by talking about how much colder it must be in Nainital.

Mother became addicted to steaming sweet-strong tea. 'It's the only thing that keeps me going,' she would sigh, as she set the aluminium pateela on the fire for yet another glass. Sugar was expensive, and even jaggery dust, which we used, cost money. Mother abandoned her usual frugality and recklessly kept buying tea and jaggery from Shrikrishnji's shop. One day she returned holding up her purchases, looking flushed and a little defiant. 'Don't stop me from having this tea,' she said, 'it's my only indulgence.'

I was never an observant child, and did not pay any attention to the subtle changes that began overtaking her towards the end of that bitter winter. Her skin seemed to regain an earlier, remembered sheen, and the fine nest of wrinkles around her eyes all but disappeared. Her gait, too, had changed; there was a rhythm to it that nobody who knew anything about these things could have missed. I concluded that the early spring and sunny mid-afternoons were responsible for her change in colour.

The plum and apricot trees were in blossom, and the sky was a clear, triumphant blue. The days were getting warmer, there was something gentle and invigorating about the fragrant March breeze, and a part of the anxiety and dread that I carried like a secret burden seemed to be gradually disappearing with the spring.

One sunny afternoon I set off as usual to collect firewood from the woods behind our house. It was a Saturday. After I came back from school I had whiled away the mid-morning sharpening my precious lead pencils with an old knife. A sharpened pencil gave me an immense sense of satisfaction, and I used to collect the pencil shavings in a cardboard box, certain that I would someday find a practical use for them.

I decided that the woods smelt like my box of pencil shavings, and the thought made me happy. I set about industriously gathering a neat heap of strong dry twigs, ideal for kindling, and then began looking for pine cones. I was obsessed by pine cones, and had squirrelled away hundreds of them in the little shack beside our outdoor privy.

'What are they for?' my mother had asked me suspiciously when the pile became too big to be ignored as a child's diversion.

'I'm going to build a palace,' I replied disingenuously, 'a palace of pine cones. We can even live there. It will be warm and cosy in winter, and if I paint the pine cones golden everyone will think we are very rich.' Although I knew this was nonsense, a part of me believed what I was saying; it sounded logical.

Mother replied by way of a resounding slap.

I looked at her in dismay. I wasn't used to being slapped, for Mother managed to maintain a strenuous discipline without the use of force. She was not being cruel, it was just that my stupid talk probably irritated her. She didn't say anything after that, she simply stomped away in disgust.

I have always been a stubborn person, and I resolved to put together the world's largest collection of pine cones. Even if a palace of pine cones was not really a workable idea, I would find some other sensible use for them. Mother would realize how wrong she had been and repent. She would apologize for that slap, and I would forgive her.

That Saturday afternoon, as I was heaping the pine cones into a large gunny bag I had stolen from the kirana store, a sharp wind stirred through the trees and the sun was swept under a procession of wrathful clouds. An angry drizzle gave way to a furious hail storm, and the firewood I had gathered with so much effort turned damp and useless. I was drenched to the bone, and the hail stones had begun to hurt. I piled up the pine cones under a spreading oak tree, and covered myself with the gunny bag, using it as a makeshift cloak.

The sky was forked by jagged lightning, and the forest around me seemed suddenly silver and alive. Then two claps of thunder, followed by the cackle of manic laughter. A woman jumped off the branches of the oak tree I was sheltering under. She landed with a thud on my heap of pine cones, and sent them tumbling down the steep slope. She was tall and lean and very strange: her eyes glimmered and she smelt of tobacco, combined with a rank animal smell that made me gag. She was dressed in several layers of rags, and her hair was matted and dirty and looked as though it had not been combed in decades.

I had not seen anybody so frightening in my entire life. I turned to run, but she caught hold of me by the wrist.

'You silly girl,' she said, 'you're young and pretty just now, but remember, soon, very soon, you'll become just like me!'

I began to whimper. Waves of terror held me rooted to the spot, though she had let go of me by now. 'Your teeth will fall away,' she whispered, 'and your hair too! I was young and pretty once, but look at me now!' She let loose her already dishevelled hair with a wild movement, and, bending forward, waved it like a mane before me.

Then she got down on all fours and began searching for something in the wet undergrowth. She found two acorn caps, which she fitted dexterously onto the nails of her index fingers. 'Look at me now!' she said in a sing-song voice. 'I'm a tree, I'm not a flower any more. That's the only way. Remember that, little girl! Now you can go.' She clambered back onto the tree with the lithe agility of a young leopard.

I rushed to the remaining pine cones and stuffed them into the soaking gunny bag. Abandoning the damp firewood, I ran all the way home, stumbling over stones and boulders, tripping over tree roots.

The terror of that afternoon has remained coiled in my heart, and through every action of every hour of my life, I have been aware of it. That was the day I realized I was doomed. I had nothing to gain in life; only to lose. I would become like her. My hair would fall off, and my teeth as well, for her madness had called out to mine.

Mother was not home when I returned. I went down to the kirana shop and found it locked. As I was turning back

I heard scurrying sounds coming from within. I decided that they were from the mice for which Shrikrishnji's shop was infamous. Disgruntled customers had complained about suspicious-looking droppings in the sugar and the rice. Then I heard the unmistakable sound of a woman's laughter. Because I had never before heard my mother laugh, I did not realize at that time that it was her.

But the sound of that laughter began haunting me. I noticed that the shop was now frequently shut in the afternoons: the thick wooden doors were bolted from within. I began hanging around the shop after school. I would pretend to leave to gather firewood, and, quickly retracing my steps, return to the shop and mount a watch. I would hear the sounds of scuffling, and the woman's laugh, and Shrikrishnji's voice sounding oddly different behind the locked doors. An all-consuming curiosity took possession of me, and one day I found myself balancing precariously on a pile of rubbish, peeping in through a broken side window.

I have never understood why, but I was not at all surprised to see my mother in Shrikrishnji's arms. They seemed very happy and intimate together. There was a lot of tickling and giggling and laughter. The shopkeeper extracted a liquor bottle from his coat pocket and glugged a good part of it down. Then, only half-jokingly, he offered it to Mother. To my absolute horror, she took it, and, giggling like a schoolgirl, actually put it to her lips and drank.

My world was shattered. People were not as they appeared. There was another life behind their masks. These cavorting figures were no better than ghosts—they belonged to a nightmare. I shut my eyes tightly, willing them to disappear, but they were no wraiths; my mother and our tenant stood before me in the flesh, their true nature unmasked.

I slunk away from the window. A sort of film descended over my eyes, and I had a strong sensation of being physically lifted and removed from within myself. Years later, when I was wheeled in for surgery from the asylum in Bareilly, I experienced the same sensation when I went under anaesthesia.

However, I continued with my everyday chores, collecting firewood, making tea, even stopping to admire the plum trees in blossom. There was nothing out of the ordinary in my mother's behaviour, and I too maintained a careful calm. There was no way I could confront her with what I had seen. In any case, I had decided that although they looked similar, my mother and the woman downstairs were two different people. Only at night, when it was time to sleep, did I try to investigate the truth. I lay down next to Mother in bed. Putting my arms around her, I tried cautiously to sniff out any liquor smells that might still be clinging to her. But she smelt of lemon and mint and other fragrant things, and I was even more convinced that it was her shadow, her evil twin, that I had glimpsed downstairs.

I became obsessed by the window, and spent long afternoons watching the masquerading spirit that had overpowered my mother, observing her heightened colour, her youthful gait, and her silly behaviour with a lecherous old shopkeeper. A spiteful voice kept insinuating strange things to me, and sometimes a bright light spread over my eyes like a flash and blinded me to what I saw. Mother and I were both very careful with each other now. I discovered a great capacity for deception, and told elaborate stories about how I planned to spend the afternoon, so that she would further let her guard down when I settled myself at the window.

The flashing lights that came and went from the corner of my eyes became more frequent. The sly voice that slandered my mother proliferated into many voices, and unknown people conducted long debates and got into heated arguments inside my head.

Both of us became used to this state of affairs. No one else ever came to know. When I glimpsed Shrikrishnji, seated behind the heaped-up rice, leaning lazily on a sack of sugar, I did not betray any agitation. On the contrary I made it a point to chat with him, about school, or the weather, or bee-keeping—to his surprise, for this was uncharacteristic—until mother reproved me for getting too familiar.

The girls at school talked incessantly about daayans and witches and evil spirits that entered the bodies of perfectly normal folks. The greatest danger, they stressed, was for the invading spirit to be found out. If and when confronted, the spirit would completely destroy the body of the hapless human it was occupying. I decided to be very careful, never to confront the spirit that possessed my mother, for I did not want her to die.

I began to have nightmares. I would wake up, trembling, drenched in sweat, and toss and turn in bed until the dawn broke. I had a recurring dream where I was bound and gagged and thrown down a steep cliff at midnight. The feeling of weightlessness, of falling, of hurtling through space, would overcome me and I would awake with a thud. One night I awoke, gasping and choking, to find that she was not in the room. After a while she returned, smiling secretively. I thought I could smell the faint reek of liquor, but I could not be sure. I was certain it was the evil twin, my mother's shade, who was in the room with me. 'Parvati,' the daayan whispered, 'come and lie down with me, Parvati.'

I pretended to be asleep, to will her away, but she came over to my bed and stroked my brow. I grew rigid with fear, and broke into a shrill scream. There was a flash of lightning outside, and in the dark I saw my mother's face, a mask of deceit; there was a roll of thunder, and the sound of the rain on the tin roof silenced my screams.

My mother could not understand the change in me. I had become even more withdrawn, there were dark circles under my eyes and I would tremble at the slightest sound. School was out of the question. I did not even venture downstairs any more, except to go to the privy in the backyard. My mother coaxed me to eat bananas, which somebody had told her were good for the nerves, and she would cook khichdi and jawla for me, which I would refuse to eat.

The following winter Shrikrishnji decided to shut his shop for two months and go to the plains. It was too cold in the hills, he said, and he had some pressing work in Bombay. After his departure, things began to heal between my mother and me. She began to look as she had used to: the lines around her eyes returned, and she was suddenly older, thinner, more fragile than she had ever been.

We rarely went to Nainital. My uncle ran a bachelor household, where he had made it amply clear we were not welcome. Mother asked me if I wanted to visit him. I told her that Nainital was probably even colder than Jeolikote, whatever would we do there? But she continued to drop all kinds of little hints, until I found us at the bus stop in Nainital, looking up in awe at the black thunder clouds clustered around China Peak. It began raining furiously. We were drenched, and took shelter under the rickshaw stand. My uncle's house was impossibly far away. We had nowhere to go, and I was not at all sure why we had come to Nainital in the first place. My mother was looking feverish, she was coughing, there was a wheezy edge to her voice when she spoke. She looked nervous and unsure of herself.

Sheets of rain were pouring down upon us. I didn't know what to do. We walked into a sports shop, where I stared at cricket bats and badminton rackets and shuttlecocks and wondered confusedly about their possible use. When the rain stopped we took the bus back to Jeolikote. I cooked dinner for us, but Mother wouldn't eat. I persuaded her to have a glass of warm milk, and sat beside her all night, while she coughed and wheezed and wept.

She ran a high fever for a week, but refused to call the doctor. I nursed her devotedly. I thought she was getting better, but then she took ill again, and developed a rasping cough which wouldn't leave. The local doctor had gone to Haldwani, but the compounder sahib came and gave her an injection.

When the doctor returned from Haldwani it was diagnosed that she had tuberculosis. That accounted for her flushed good looks and heightened colour. I wondered if her illness had resulted from my shameless spying; perhaps the spirit which possessed her had chosen to destroy her upon being found out.

Her stepbrother Hiranandji came down to Jeolikote from

Nainital and conferred with the doctor. It was decided that
Mother was to be moved to the TB sanatorium in Bhowali.
It was an expensive place, Kamla Nehru had been treated
there, but Masterji waved such considerations aside and told
us loftily that he would never be wanting in the execution
of his duties. He escorted her all the way to Bhowali, and
assured me gravely that everything was going to be all right.
His promises rang hollow in my ears. I was sent to stay
overnight with Lata Sah, in their bungalow. When her
mother held me in her arms her gold and glass bangles flashed
and tinkled, and I thought of my mother's work-worn hands
and let loose a few sour and exhausted tears. I knew that
she was going to die and I was deeply shamed by my lack of
sorrow. I was worried and watchful, but I had no grieving
to offer.

I knew that my life would change after she died. My
uncle's house was a sahib's house with servants and sofas,
and I looked forward to the day I would get to live there.
Quite seriously I assured Lata Sah that she and her mother
were welcome to visit us anytime, once I had moved in with
my uncle.

*

A chaprasi from the school escorted me from Jeolikote to
Nainital. The house was an odd-looking cottage called 'Wee
Nooke'. It was situated a short distance away from the main
school buildings. My uncle made me feel welcome and I felt
secure that the hostility he had felt for his stepsister did not
extend to me.

Masterji was several years older than my mother. He
had never married. It was rumoured that he had taken a

vow of chastity after reading the collected works of Swami Vivekananda. He was a thin, stern man with a kind smile. I found his habitual silence reassuring and he seemed relieved by my lack of conversation.

I assumed the part of a young lady with natural ease. I was to study in the GGIC, which was the acronym for the Government Girls Inter College. I had a new blue-and-white salwar suit, which was the official school uniform, and crisp new ribbons for my hair.

I remember those years in Nainital as times of dazzling sunshine, without shadows or fears. Penury had trained me well, and I took over the running of the household with practised ease. I discovered that the maidservant who lived in the outhouse was a Muslim. This did not shock me, and after I had carefully examined her sympathetic face I was reassured to find that she did not wear a mask.

I enjoyed a certain status in the eyes of the masters and teachers who occasionally visited us, and basked in their polite attentions. I even became friendly with some of the students. One of them, Masterji's particular favourite, was a tongue-tied young man called Mukul Nainwal. He looked at me with undisguised adoration, and gradually I began to see myself through his eyes, as a beautiful young woman. The Parvati who had lived with her mother in Jeolikote had receded deep into the past, and a merry young creature had set up camp inside me.

I hardly recognized this new Parvati. She intimidated me a little; she was given to trilling laughter and sudden fits of sadness and her eyes glittered with nervous energy whenever I surprised her reflection in the mirror.

I was preoccupied with my physical self. I blotted my

lips with geranium petals to make them red and bought myself an eyebrow pencil to augment my scanty brows. I even tried to induce a beauty spot on my right cheek, using a combination of black ink and eyebrow pencil, but my terror of Masterji prevailed and I washed it off before the world could witness the transformation.

It was in this state I first saw Salman, and I was dazzled by his beauty. I could immediately sense that Salman wore a mask, but the knowledge excited and challenged me. We knew when our eyes met that we were ancient partners, and our shadows embraced right there in the middle of Masterji's drawing room.

Salman Siddiqui taught history to the senior classes. He had a pale ivory skin, and an air of composure and confidence that seemed destined for a larger world than Nainital. Very soon I was pestering Masterji for help with my history homework. Of course he did not have the time, though he did at first try his best to help out. After a particularly tedious session, when I persisted in seeking the most trivial and enervating clarifications, he snapped, as I had known he would. 'Why don't you ask Mr Siddiqui,' he said, 'he loves teaching history.'

Had my mother still been alive she might have expressed some doubts about an impressionable young girl being taught history by a young man of such exceptional beauty. But Masterji, who kept a Muslim maidservant and had himself taken a vow of chastity after reading Vivekananda, was above such mundane concerns.

'Awake, arise, and stop not till the goal is reached,' he said, almost absent-mindedly, one afternoon as he left us alone in the drawing room at Wee Nooke to pursue the study of history. Salman did not put up any pretence of teaching me; he pulled me into his arms and we tumbled into a long, passionate kiss. My whole body seemed to soar into a new, separate plane of being. The texture of Salman's mouth in mine, the thumping of our two hearts, united for those few minutes into a single, simple beat—nothing in my life, no previous joy or pleasure, had prepared me for my first kiss.

I was caught completely unawares by the devastating bliss. Eating a sweet squelchy gulabjamun, biting into a fresh fragrant apple, clambering up a khumani tree, with the blue sky above and the hard pliant branch beneath my legs, pretending I was riding a horse—nothing in my meagre experience of physical pleasures had ever predicted such ecstasy.

With the recklessness that I was to later recognize as so uniquely his, Salman attacked my sari blouse and began pulling at the hooks with an urgency so total that my blouse fell open almost of its own accord. By now my entire body was afire, all discretion had abandoned me. I clung desperately to him. The searing look in his eyes cleft all the way into my soul.

I was hurtling towards disaster, but of course I didn't care. Salman, with the sixth sense of the dedicatedly amorous, heard the click of the key on the front door and pulled himself away from my hungry lips with the ease of an athlete at play. I was still fumbling with my sari when Masterji strode into the room, and gazed at us with benign approval. 'Ah, busy with studies, I see,' he said, and left us alone again, indicating his satisfaction with a discreet cough before he left.

Salman grabbed my hand as soon as Masterji had left. 'We mustn't be found out,' I said, pulling away. 'Why don't you teach me some history?'

Salman seemed to enjoy teaching me history almost as much as he seemed to enjoy kissing me. Together we explored the past. In some unspecified future, Salman planned to specialize in European history. His eyes lit up when he spoke of the Moorish influences in European architecture, or as he explained the convoluted history of Christianity. He was particularly enamoured of Spanish history. He would talk to me of conquistadors and Mamelukes and the plunder of gold and silver from far continents. I would listen enthralled, understanding little of what he said, fascinated by the foreign names. Sometimes he would be so lost in talk that he would even let go of my hand, which he otherwise held with passionate intensity through the length of his discourses.

His lessons were of no use to me: the history of the world as taught in the Government Girls Inter College differed radically in its concepts from Salman's world view. Moreover, we had to write our answer sheets in Hindi, in which even the names of people and places were quite different. Aristotle was 'Aristoo', Plato was 'Aflatoon', and Alexander was 'Sikander'. In a strictly academic sense, Salman's lessons only served to confuse me, although they did arouse a quite unprecedented passion for the past in my mind.

The only comparable experience I had was my brief but intense involvement with the fundamentals of bee-keeping, and in an act of mental barter, I told Salman all that I knew about the species Hymenoptera; about the dance of the honeybee as she searches for food and pastures and pollen:

how she returns to tell her friends of what she has found—the round dance if sustenance is nearby, otherwise the 'tail wag' to tell them what to do and where to go.

'Does she tell them what not to do?' he asked mischievously, his hands ardent and eager in their busy pursuits.

My hymen was still intact, although I was getting increasingly agitated about its expeditious disposal. I was however more prudent than Salman, who would have had his way with me right there under Masterji's nose. I counselled patience, and we contented ourselves with stolen kisses and amorous looks.

Modern history left Salman quite unmoved. As a Muslim, he felt alienated from both Pakistan, where his father and sister had fled shortly after Partition, some ten years ago, and the New India. His ambition was to leave India, and start anew in another country. 'History in the making is never as interesting as the detached study of an absolute past,' he said. He had his arms around my waist, and I could feel his warm breath upon my neck. I compared the colour of our skins; Salman was undoubtedly the fairer, and the curly black hair on his arms made me shudder with desire.

When the rains came I fell seriously ill. I was diagnosed with typhoid fever. I was a bad patient and Munnibee, the maidservant, declared herself frankly not up to the task of looking after me.

The doctor agreed that I would be best off in hospital. Masterji was glad to have me off his hands. I found myself in a miraculous new environment, one where soft fluffed-up pillows and clean fragrant bedsheets were transposed with the sounds and smells of the monsoon rain on the roof and the thick pale fog that rolled right into the room. The Ramsay hospital had been built by Englishmen for Englishmen. Its polished floors and beautifully arranged flowers left me speechless. I felt as though I was trespassing in a cathedral. My debilitated condition had also weakened my mind, and I wondered sometimes if I were already dead, and inhabiting some kind of sensual paradise. As typhoid was considered highly infectious, I was not placed in the general wards, but given a room to myself. The nurses were all Anglo-Indians; I suspected them of being angels and the efficient clink of thermometer on glass was as musical to my ears as any heavenly choir.

The matron at the Ramsay hospital was one Sister Louise Dickens. She was kind and concerned about the patients, even the Indians who had of late begun to frequent the hospital, but she was an absolute dragon when it came to visitors. Visiting hours were strictly adhered to, and when the time was up she would move from room to room and sternly reprimand any dawdlers, even the white memsahibs who came with bunches of lilies in their arms.

I had no visitors, although Masterji kept a diligent check on my progress. A week after I had been admitted to hospital, I was woken from my sleep by the electric touch of a familiar hand. Light streamed into the room from the hospital corridors, and I could discern the unnaturally handsome contours of Salman's face as it floated with an angelic luminosity above mine. I decided that this was either a dream, or that I had died and been transported to heaven, for there was no earthly way in which Salman could have countermanded Sister Louise Dickens' visiting hours and materialized in my room. In neither case was I responsible or culpable. I abandoned myself to whatever was to be.

Although we had kissed and fondled each other, and I had known and recognized the knot of joy he carried with him, I was still unprepared for the piercing pain of penetration, the reactivation of the womb, the agony of that knowledge. As I succumbed to the rhythm of Salman's body within mine I knew paradise.

I had never imagined that the human body could be the instrument of such delights. Underneath the sterilized white sheets I was dressed in a hospital robe, which was most convenient for our purposes. I could feel his warm breath travelling across my neck, my collarbones, my breasts. Convulsions of joy rippled through my body, shudders of anticipation and delight, like waves on the lake, each merging into the other, faster and faster, like an April storm, and then, a streak of lightning and the sound of thunder and the rain falling into the lake and seeping through the valley.

*

By the morning he was gone, and when the nurse came in to take my temperature there was no sign of our nocturnal revels. Salman visited me every night after that, he would corporealize sometime after midnight surrounded by fog and mist and darkness. I was getting rapidly better, although I was in no hurry to recover and return home. The nurses all commented on my glowing looks, even the normally dour matron told me that I was looking like 'an angel from heaven'. I had not forsaken the conviction that I had indeed accidently landed in some other dimension. When, in all seriousness, I told Salman of this, he laughed and told me of the Assassins, who were on the appointed day given prodigious quantities of hashish and taken to a paradisiacal garden, which, they were assured, would be their certain destination were their murderous missions to misfire.

I had left Wee Nooke a girl, I returned a woman. I realized that we had to cover our tracks very carefully, for, liberal as Masterji might be, he was a man of his times, and, like most celibate men, a prude. He was unlikely to encourage a romance, leave alone a torrid affair, between his niece and a young Muslim boy, however good a history teacher he may have been.

My mother was atypical in that she had completely lacked in religious feeling. She always looked more than a little scornful when confronted with the pious sentiments of our Jeolikote neighbours. 'If I ever meet that old man, God, I'll tell him what I really think of him!' she would say. 'If I've survived, it's in spite, not because, of the old so-and-so...!' My view of tradition and religion was influenced by hers. The fact that I was a Hindu Brahmin girl and Salman a Muslim did not therefore strike me as any impediment to our union. However, although he was most enthusiastic about getting his hands on me whenever possible, Salman never talked of a future or of a life together. We were playing a shadow game, and the most precious ingredient of our passion was that the both of us sensed that it was not permanent.

During the period of my convalescence in Wee Nooke, I impressed upon Salman the need for secrecy. I advised him level-headedly to curb his ardour, for he would certainly lose his job if Masterji came to know, and moreover, in all likelihood not get a reference either.

We managed with great difficulty to keep apart from

each other. My days and nights passed in sweet yearning. I read poetry. Mukul Nainwal waited upon me devotedly. I played the role of a demure young girl with consummate artistry. I could dissemble with ease before Mukul Nainwal and his friend Lalit Joshi, and Masterji's academic preoccupations left him with little time for human affairs. The only person I could not fool was the maidservant, Munnibee. She was a woman; I could sense that she saw through the simpering pose of my sickness to the secret glow within.

I did not hear from Salman for a long time. One afternoon, I overheard Mukul and Lalit excitedly discussing their history teacher. I knew that both of them had something of a crush on Salman, his effulgent good looks could leave no one untouched.

'He's disappeared,' they were saying, 'he's simply vanished into thin air.'

'Like Houdini,' Lalit said solemnly. 'I heard he's gone to Bombay.'

'No, Baltimore, somewhere in America.'

I listened half curiously. I had never suspected Salman of permanence. I had known in our very first meeting that he was only a shadow.

Munnibee volunteered further information. Salman had been meeting an Anglo-Indian nurse at the Ramsay hospital; they were having an affair. The nurse had slashed her wrists, her condition was critical, she had been rushed to Bareilly for treatment. The matron was furious; it was a scandal, everyone was talking about it.

Masterji kept a studied silence about the whole episode. A few months later, a letter arrived from Bombay. Salman wrote to us, apologizing for his abrupt departure; his mother had suddenly taken ill. Circumstances compelled him to stay on in Bombay. He was contemplating a move to America, where his sister was now settled.

I was stoic, even relieved, about his departure. A part of me had recognized the risks I was taking. My encounter with Salman had quelled some silent hunger within me. I felt triumphantly normal, and indeed the next few years were probably the happiest in my life.

I enjoyed flirting with Mukul Nainwal. His absolute adoration and the transparent ploys he employed to be with me were balm to my soul. My studies kept me busy, and then there was the housekeeping. I discovered that I was good with my hands; I knitted a sweater for Masterji, a scarf for Mukul, a shawl for myself. I was immersed in daily life, and although I did not have many friends in school, I was not unpopular.

I went to the cinema with Mukul and Lalit, and to picnics with my friends, where we sang songs and laughed a lot and came home exhausted. My nervous energy was building up again, and I was certain it was happiness.

The year I turned twenty Masterji told me that I was to be married. He had chosen a boy for me, somebody I already knew, and obviously liked. I thought perhaps he was talking about Mukul Nainwal, who had by then moved to Allahabad for higher studies; but no, Masterji had decided that I was to be married to Mukul's best friend, Lalit Joshi.

It was not that I disliked Lalit, in fact, all in all, I rather liked him. But Masterji could not be expected to understand that I was a woman, and Lalit was, in my eyes, still a boy. Though, after Salman's departure matters sexual had begun to fill me with a sort of belated shame, I still missed him, I missed the physical journeys we had undertaken together. Salman had not considered me important enough to stay on for, he had not even bothered to bid me goodbye. His rejection didn't hurt me, I could bear the pain, but it had diminished me.

I considered the prospect of marriage to Lalit. It was not likely to be very exciting, but I was hardly in any position to contradict Masterji or his decision. Lalit was a Brahmin like me, our horoscopes and our gotras matched: we were not related to each other, as was so often the case with Kumaoni Brahmins. Moreover, Masterji wanted me off his hands. He had done his duty, and it was time for me to do mine.

A few odd relatives did somehow manage to make themselves manifest for the marriage ceremonies. Lalit had a large and loving family; I winced at the very sight of their gregarious confabulations. Masterji's nephew, Pooran, his great-aunt, Lachibubu, and his mother's cousins constituted the celebrants from our side. Masterji asked if there was anyone I wished to invite. I thought suddenly of my friend Lata Sah in Jeolikote, and her mother who had always been so kind to me. A few girls in my class, and a card to Mukul, forwarded to Allahabad—there were not more than six people I could think of inviting.

The day I was to be married I was ritually bathed with turmeric and sandalwood. I wore a red silk sari and the gold champakali necklace my mother had left me.

After the sexual bliss I had known with Salman, my wedding night with Lalit sent us both into the deepest depression. We were escorted into a small mean room by a battalion of giggling relatives. The bed itself, part of the dowry Masterji had munificently provided, was an elaborate affair ordered from Haldwani through the sports teacher whose father owned a furniture shop there. Already, inexplicably, the woven newar mattress was sagging in the centre. We had both seen enough Hindi films to know what was expected of us. The decorum of the occasion demanded languishing looks, a tender appraisal of the bride by the eager bridegroom, and then, hopefully, down to business. I had tasted real passion, and I could feel nothing but scorn for this farce. My young husband looked puzzled, even oppressed, and kept a stubborn, watchful distance from me.

Lalit had always trailed after his friend Mukul Nainwal, admiring him in all he did. I had somehow assumed that I would be able to demand of him the same homage that Mukul so unstintingly proffered. It came as something of a disagreeable shock to realize that he was as unenthusiastic about our nuptials as I was.

The pressures only escalated with time. A bitter silence built up between us those waiting nights. Months passed and the reluctant bridegroom still did not get down to his duties. I began to suffer from constipation and a ceaseless mounting tension.

I was expected to cook for Lalit's family. Here I was able to display my culinary prowess, and took some satisfaction from the praise all of them heaped on me. As I got to know them better I grew to like them as an affectionate, trusting lot. I was undeservedly popular with them: Parvati bhabhi was considered an accomplished and dashing new addition to the extended family.

I found it unpleasant to live in such close proximity to a man. Lalit was not very clean in his personal habits, and a dank, stale smell of sweat sat upon his body. It rose like a miasma from his clothes when I washed them, the very memory of it made me gag. At night we slept beside each other on the narrow bed like hostile strangers. Sometimes by accident his hand brushed against mine, or my leg would entangle with his. We both treated such chance encounters with cold courtesy.

I had grown up a solitary child. Life within the fabric of a joint family was so tightly enmeshed that the opportunities for us to know or understand each other were extremely limited. My numerous nieces and nephews-in-law, who were always romping around the small house, became my friends and confidantes. I began to encourage them to even sleep in our room: their presence was an effective shield against the cold hostility of our nights together.

During our time in Wee Nooke, when Mukul, Lalit and I had been bonded in friendship, I had felt safe and secure in our camaraderie. After our marriage, after I became Mrs Lalit Joshi, I realized that the stubborn hostility that Lalit harboured towards me could not have developed overnight; it had its roots in those happy days at Wee Nooke: he must surely have hated me even then. Gradually, this hatred seeped osmotically into my system, and became both a verdict and a sentence.

A year after we were married, we moved to the plains. Bareilly was hot and dusty and ugly and fascinating and I hoped against hope that a change of scene might improve things between us.

Soon after our arrival in Bareilly we received a letter from Mukul Nainwal. It was addressed to both of us—Mr & Mrs Lalit Joshi. I opened it eagerly. Just the sight of Mukul's tidy italic hand made me feel more human. He was full of himself and his new job; his small vanities rose like familiar emanations from the lined notepaper; the letter transported me to happier, more innocent times. Mukul was planning to visit Bareilly in the course of an 'official tour', and he hoped that we could all spend some time together.

That afternoon I braided my hair carefully into a double plait. A popular film tune rose unbidden to my lips. Lalit returned home late from office. After he had his tea, and made his ritual sojourn to the latrine, after he had had taken off his battered shoes and stuffed his faintly smelly socks inside them, he found the letter lying on my dressing table. The expression of delight when he recognized Mukul's handwriting quickly changed to an unfathomable rage. The look in his eyes when he turned to face me made me wince, and his slap sent me hurtling across the small room. I fell over the cheap wooden settee; as I struggled to get up he made for me again.

'How dare you!' he screamed, his eyes dilated with anger and hatred. 'You prying whore!'

Just then our next-door neighbours, a couple from Ratlam, knocked at the door. They were in the habit of dropping in once or twice a week; their timely visit served for the moment to defuse Lalit's inexplicable anger. By the next morning he seemed to have forgotten all about it; we never discussed the matter again.

A sense of physical, bodily fear took hold of me. From that night I began to spread the spare mattress on the floor, preferring to sleep there rather than risk even an accidental encounter with Lalit's scathing, hostile presence. I had been married for over a year, but we were no nearer to consummating our marriage, and by now I had become reconciled to the idea that we never would. I wondered if this was God's punishment for my sluttish behaviour with Salman, or if the sins of my mother were being visited on me.

A week later Mukul arrived in a haze of glory, in his official jeep, accompanied by a liveried attendant. The woman in me had asserted herself, and I had taken special care to look beautiful. Mukul's wholehearted adoration was balm to my wounds: I turned to gauge Lalit's reaction, vaguely hopeful that jealousy would provoke him towards the biological conclusion for which, in spite of everything, I was physically longing. As my demure downcast eyes darted towards my husband, I was indeed surprised to see the most undisguised jealousy in his. For a moment my spirits lifted. Then the truth registered, and I realized that I had blundered my way into a nightmare; for the jealousy was mixed with an expression of intense yearning, which was directed not towards me but Mukul.

The very air in our living room was crackling with sexual static. Seemingly oblivious to Lalit's looks, Mukul stared at me ardently. The spite that lit up Lalit's otherwise phlegmatic face made it for the moment potent, even strong. My terror, a familiar terror, one I had encountered earlier, I recognized from the time I had stumbled upon my mother laughing in the shopkeeper Shrikrishnji's arms.

If there is any one moment in my life I consider axial, on which all its other movements and motions hinge, it was this one, when I encountered my husband, Lalit, look at Mukul with hunger in his eyes. The mask of lust sat taut upon his ordinary face; the telltale twitch near his mouth made him appear both pathetic and obscene. I thought of those long-ago days in Nainital, when the two of them had attended upon me like pageboys and paid me homage; when I was a princess and Salman my prince. Which one of us would have foreseen this corruption of hope and happiness?

The very hair on my arms stood on end as I understood the implications of what I was witnessing. Everything about the past year fell swiftly and precisely into place.

Nothing I knew or understood could have led me to put such a lewd construct on their noble and passionate friendship. But thirteen months of unfulfilled marriage, when I had lived like a prisoner of war, constantly spying on the habits and inclinations of my captor, had given me an instinctive understanding of my husband. I knew now with a sense of numbing finality that it was so, and so it would remain.

Never quick on the uptake, Mukul was continuing with his painstaking bragging; there was a pleading in his eyes, a silence, a question, that mutely and yet eloquently demanded not an answer but an absolution.

It was in his eyes that I received my answer. I was defined, formulated, forgiven: I was a Hindu woman, a married woman. I would tenaciously live out the role, safe in its stern unremitting code. If I performed the motions with enough fluency and ease, then perhaps within the confines of my neglected womb, I would find the inner space, the private territory, the strength to stage and execute a very private revolt.

I made koftas for dinner, employing a special recipe that involved the use of khus-khus, which our neighbour from Ratlam had taught me. The terror and tension of our first encounter passed; the three of us de-escalated abruptly into our old undemanding friendship. We joked and laughed and remembered old times; we saw a film together at the new cinema hall, we went for a drive along the river front in Mukul's jeep. Not once did his hand reach out for my arm, or his touch linger at my elbow; not once did I look him in the eyes, or in any way answer the questions they posed. Sometimes the gajra of fresh young chameli flowers in my hair, the warm summer smells of earth and water and night, aroused me to a fever of expectation and desire, but I did not give in, I cooked and smiled and wore my new frozen face to such perfection that I understood resignedly that it had been made to measure and that I was condemned to wear it for a very long time, perhaps forever.

When Mukul went away, on to a new posting and an exciting new life, we returned once again to sleeping in our separate beds; the only difference being that I prudently moved my mattress out to the kitchen, for the roaches and mice that lived there seemed less hostile than Lalit. My husband made no comment on the new arrangement; we had expeditiously reduced the necessary level of communication to the very barest minimum. Days, weeks would pass in bitter, brooding silence, broken only by innocent visits from the garrulous couple from Ratlam, when we too would put up a front of normalcy and even happiness.

My silence, my calm, as I sleepwalked through this unexpected role, was construed by our happy group as the praiseworthy reticence normal to the Indian woman, it aroused no questions or comments.

The occasional letters from Masterji, in his usual spidery scrawl, were full of homilies about my duties as a wife and a woman. 'I trust,' he wrote, with a note of prophetic warning, 'that you will never display that over-masculine approach to life which your dear departed mother sometimes demonstrated.'

Everybody in Lalit's family was waiting for some 'good news': the surfeit of nieces and nephews that swarmed about their Nainital home had evidently not satisfied my in-laws' desire for progeny. It did not surprise me that they sensed nothing of the tragic absurdity of our lives. They did not notice, for instance, that I had grown slatternly about my looks; I no longer took the trouble to oil my long hair or to comb it down. I was increasingly indifferent about my clothes and the soles of my feet had become so cracked that I found it difficult to even walk around the house.

Only my culinary skills had not abandoned me. I delighted in making the most elaborate meals, which Lalit ate without comment. It was evident that he enjoyed the food, to which he sometimes accorded a grunt of bad-tempered appreciation. He was growing fatter, his features coarsened further as his waistline broadened. I felt safe when he ate my cooking, I felt it accorded me some power over his corpulent body, some part in the dreary dominion of our home.

The unmitigated silence of our lives was broken by the arrival in Bareilly of Lalit's younger brother. Raju had come to the plains in search of a job, but he was not in any way trained or qualified to earn his living. Just two years younger than Lalit, he was different from him in every way. Where my husband was thrifty, conscientious and hard-working, Raju was extravagant, lazy and charming. There was an optimism and panache in his attitude that I found heartening; he had evidently not resigned himself to the world's evaluation of him.

When Raju found me sleeping in the kitchen, surrounded by rats and vermin, he seemed not in the least surprised. 'So that's how the land lies, is it?' he grinned. 'Is this a lover's quarrel or has my respected brother's hatred of the fair sex finally asserted itself?'

I blushed furiously, wondering how much he knew. But Raju was too involved in the drama of his own life to expend time and emotion to any situation but his own. 'Never mind. *Koi baat nahi*,' he continued, 'Don't pay attention to *choti-choti baaten*, my dear bhabhiji.'

Raju did not seem to be making any real effort to find a job. After Lalit left for his office, my brother-in-law would lounge about in his loose, flappy kurta-pyjamas, following me about the house as I went about my chores, keeping me amused by his constant and irreverent banter. Later in the day he would saunter off to meet some friends, or to enquire about some vague job prospect which was always just around the corner, on the very verge of being offered to him. He was always careful to return early in the evening, and put up an earnest form before Lalit. My husband had instructed me gruffly that I was to sleep in his room now that his brother was living in the house. Sometimes, late at night, as I was staring sleeplessly at the dark figures that seemed to crowd among the cobwebs, suspended above the ceiling fan, I would hear the light click of the back door; when I crept into the kitchen at night for a nocturnal glass of water, I would find that Raju had disappeared, leaving the back door locked and bolted from the outside.

As we grew friendlier, Raju began to confide in me. 'There's only one thing I want from life,' he would say, 'and that's to become rich. In our society a rich man is forgiven anything!'

I would listen opaquely, my mind distracted between the cooking and the cleaning and the washing and the tantalizing glimpses of a larger world that Mukul Nainwal's infrequent letters provided.

'I have made up my mind,' Raju would say determinedly. 'I am not running after any niggardly job. I shall become a racketeer or a blackmarketeer, or a kidnapper! Arrey listen bhabhi, I have an even better idea! I shall become his munimji, find out his darkest secrets'—by now his eyes would be misty—'then I shall inform the income tax department about my Sethji's vile activities, and with the money I'll get as an informer I shall buy a bungalow and two wives...'

'Quiet, Raju,' I would say reprovingly, but not so deep inside my own secret mutinies flared and festered, inflamed by his infectious daydreaming.

'Achha bhabhiji, as you please! I won't become an informer! I'll simply blackmail him and live a life of ease!'

I would pretend shock, but secretly I was applauding. A teasing smile would spread across his youthful face, which, although it was not handsome, had a winsome, happy quality. 'Achha, as you say! I am your slave. I shall repent, reform; I shall open a paan shop in Bombay and stay awake and listen to the radio on Vividh Bharati all night! Satisfied?'

*

One night I could not sleep. Lalit's snoring was louder than usual, and the smell from his socks wafted towards me as I lay on the mattress, which I had spread out on the ground diagonal to our bed.

I crept out and spread my bedding on the kitchen floor. A cockroach was crawling up my leg: the sensation was not unpleasant. I brushed it away after a while and sighed deeply; my life seemed doomed to an eternity of unrelieved, silent suffering.

I heard the click of the back door opening, and the sound of Raju entering the living room. I was overcome by a physical longing so acute it almost paralyzed me. When Raju came into the kitchen for some water, I was so incapacitated by desire I could not even get up from the mattress.

Raju looked at me quizzically as he tipped the water from the clay surahi. 'So, bhabhi, back to a single bed?' he said humorously.

I did not reply, but stared fixedly at the damp cement floor. Raju went back to the living room, I could hear him move as he settled into the sofa where he slept.

I floated in a state of semi-consciousness which was not sleep; a sort of sentient death or a waking suicide, a half and half between mask and self.

As though in a dream I saw Raju walk in once again into the kitchen, the moonlight from the window haloing his tousled hair. Time stood still as he lay down beside me. I felt his cool skin against my face. I gasped in terror as our breaths met. Then, strangely, I was revived, resuscitated; boldly I reached out and held his hand. We lay together and stared at the cobwebs on the ceiling. The harsh moonlight that streamed in from the skylight lit them and made them beautiful. An urgency invaded my body; I looked at his tender young face, which was not a mask, he had not then the smell of the other; he was an ally, he was like me, we were both lonely, our needs possessed us, and we made uncompromising, uncomplicated love.

Afterwards Raju fell asleep on my mattress in the kitchen, and I had to nudge him awake and send him back to the sofa. I pondered whether to return to Lalit's room, my mind was suddenly capable of deliberation, and I decided that it was more prudent to spend the night in the kitchen, rather than run the risk of waking him up by my return. I decided it best to defy Lalit's orders and continue sleeping in the kitchen as I did before Raju came to stay with us. Lalit, of course, chose not to react.

Raju was shamefaced the morning after our night together. We did not discuss what had happened. The day passed as usual, but without our normal happy banter; there was a strain and formality in our talk. Raju did not come to my bed that night, or the next; I would hear the click of the door as he left for his nocturnal adventures, and a sense of relief would settle over me. I would sleep alone on the kitchen floor, safe in my rebellion.

I could sense that I was hurling towards a terrible and inevitable fate. The next time he came to me, a week, maybe ten days later, I resisted, but not overmuch, and soon we fell into the habit, and learnt to maintain our faces in the daytime. I felt safe with Raju. He was an ally, I could bank on him. He was, after all, not a stranger, he was my husband's brother, he was family. I reassured myself that this was no betrayal.

I began combing my hair again, I hummed to myself as I washed the clothes, the cracks on my heels were mysteriously cured. Our neighbour from Ratlam commented on my improved looks, and enquired archly whether I was at last expecting some good news.

The glow returned to my skin. I was ravenously hungry all the time, and even Lalit commented on my appetite.

Raju eventually returned to Nainital; even after his departure I continued to feel an extraordinary sense of well-being. The new Parvati, this confident and happy woman I had mysteriously become, could even cope with Lalit. When he caught me smiling, which I often did nowadays, he thought I was smiling at him. He began smiling back, he complimented me on my cooking, and a nimbus of understanding faltered suddenly between us.

We had the two of us suffered so much misery together that we were both relieved by this sudden reversal of fortune. We did not mock or question it, but timidly went along with the tide of happiness.

Sometimes when Lalit's hand accidently brushed against mine, I felt a small shiver of desire, my body awakened to his touch. I cherished the secret hope that, one day, we would have a normal marriage. Lalit was, after all, my husband. He earned for me, I cooked for him; we had been friends in our childhood. We could become lovers, confidantes, allies.

Lalit had lost some weight, and his face, normally so sallow, had recently regained colour. I wondered wistfully how it would have been if our marriage had been different. I pictured Lalit coming home with a gajra of mogra flowers; I saw us going to the paan shop together, at midnight, his arms around me; I saw him buying me beautiful saris. These were of course only daydreams; the only concession to togetherness Lalit ever made was to congratulate me on my kheer, or slurp over his lunch.

In a strange progress, I learnt to dissemble, and in the process I learnt to love. I can in retrospect honestly say that by the time he died, I had learnt to love Lalit.

We had begun to sleep together again, in the same bedroom, that is. One night I saw him smile in his sleep. It was a smile I knew and remembered, a sudden, spontaneous smile that transported me to the old days in Nainital, when Mukul and Lalit and I had been friends together. He had smiled so when he found a special-issue stamp, or when the two of them shared a joke together. His colour had changed, his face was flushed, his cheeks as red and glossy as the rosy Chaubatiya apples from Ranikhet that we used to devour together in Nainital. He was far better looking than his brother Raju—we had been childhood friends, I could not understand how things had come to this pass between us, how we had plumbed such depths of hatred. On an impulse, I reached forward and stroked his cheek. He woke up and smiled at me sleepily. My heart missed a beat. He sat up and held me by the wrist. His hands were warm. 'You have been a good wife, Parvati,' he whispered, 'a good and patient wife.' His face had turned even redder, and his breathing was short and laboured. My elation turned to alarm; I rushed to the kitchen to get him some water. When I returned he was coughing violently. His entire body was convulsed, his face a mottled shade of purple. I patted him on the back, and waited for the attack to subside. He recovered his breath, sank back on the bed, and began to breathe normally again. His face was pale as death, his eyes were looking at me beseechingly.

I turned off the light and lay down beside him. He was breathing with difficulty, as though he was labouring up a steep hill. He coughed spasmodically through the night, and slept late into the morning. I tiptoed about my household chores so as not to wake him.

Lalit's descent into the land of the diseased was as sudden as it was irrevocable. It was as though he assumed citizenship of another world. I thought at first that he had a fever, or influenza; he lay in bed, enervated, inattentive, his face sometimes a white mask, sometimes flushed and febrile. He coughed a lot, and when I washed his handkerchiefs I came across the telltale stains of blood on the caked-up phlegm and sputum.

The doctor was glassy-eyed and evasive. He suggested an X-ray, and we went all the way to Lucknow to take it. Tuberculosis makes the body transparent. There, in the dark green painted room, holding my husband's fevered hand in mine, I could, for the first time, look inside him. I saw the shadowy form of his insides, the mysterious anatomy, the defeated lungs—he was no longer opaque.

There was another doctor, a chest specialist. He was a tall thin man who looked down at us from a very great height. He looked amused by the diagnosis. 'The tubercle bacilli has struck again,' he said almost facetiously. 'Your husband has what we call "galloping consumption". There is very little medical science can do for this condition. We can only advise complete rest—mental and physical rest. He needs to breathe—clean, pure air would do him good, dry out his lungs. I am giving you a letter for the director of the Bhowali sanatorium. If you go quickly, you might save his life. Apart from that, I can promise nothing.'

I remembered the Bhowali sanatorium. My mother had died there. I looked at the doctor's face, still wreathed in an inexplicable, benevolent smile, and I knew that he had as good as certified my husband dead.

We returned to Bareilly. Lalit's family was informed of his illness. His mother came to nurse him. Raju was engaged to be married, she told me. The girl was from Bombay, her father owned a dairy farm there. Raju was going to join the family business. 'They are from a very prosperous family but the girl has no airs at all,' she said. 'Although she is convented, she is really homely. Raju is very lucky.'

I kept silent. The news did not affect me in any way. It did not make me sad or happy. I did not even miss Raju or wonder how he was. It was as though he was a complete stranger. 'I think Lalit is calling for me,' I said stonily.

We tried very hard to raise money for the Bhowali sanatorium. My father-in-law, the postmaster, tried to get a loan from some relatives. Lalit wrote a letter to his boss in the factory. We received a reply saying that the management was 'considering' the request. I wrote a letter to Masterji, and another to Mukul Nainwal, asking for help. But before I could post either of them, Lalit had died. He vomited blood; it spouted from his mouth like a fountain. By the time we reached the local hospital, he was dead.

What surprised me about death was this: the soul departs, leaving the body forlorn. The body departs, it is taken away, disposed of, it disintegrates, decomposes, it is gone. The ashes are thrown into muddy rivers, the crows come and eat the sacrificial rice, and on the thirteenth day even the lamp that guides the spirit to the other world is extinguished. But things remain. Lalit's razor, with the thick stubborn growth still sticking to the blade, the handle worn with use. His shaving cream, and the limp defeated shaving brush. His nail cutter, a gift from his father, sits safely in the steel box that also holds his watch and wallet. His slippers still lie under the bed, waiting. They did not perish with him. His two suits hang in the cupboard, his shirts lie folded, quiescent. I wonder if they remember him, his smell, his body.

Thinking of this, I can only conclude that death is not final. It is an adversary, an unequal one, and the victors in this battle are rocks and stones. And razors. And wristwatches, even if they have not been wound up, and lie coiled like mortally wounded snakes in steel boxes, next to cheap leather wallets from which the notes have been removed, though not the coins, and squeezed-out tubes of shaving cream. These are my views on mortality.

And there is another thing. Death does not make us think of death: death urges us towards life.

Lalit's death and Raju's wedding are horribly mixed up in my mind, a blur of weeping and laughter, death and merriment. Lalit's family was unexpectedly affectionate and looked after me tenderly. I felt extremely sick throughout the thirteen days of ritual mourning. I was throwing up regularly, and on the sixth day, after his death, as I was tending the lamp, I fell into a dead faint. 'She is under strain,' my mother-in-law said sagely, and told me to get some rest.

They had decided not to delay Raju's marriage because of Lalit's death. His father-in-law to be was a heart patient, and he was in a hurry to get his daughter married. When Lalit's family went to Bombay with the baraat, I moved back to my uncle Hiranand Headmaster's house. I was making tea for him one afternoon when I fainted again. I was rushed to the Ramsay hospital. I remember that it was during the monsoons, the hydrangeas were in bloom, and orange-and-black-flecked tiger lilies flamed in the untiring rain. The aborted foetus in the bottle of green brine still adorned the civil surgeon's consulting room. The matron and the doctor checked my pulse, and poked around my stomach. The doctor put on plastic gloves and put his fingers up my insides. 'Congratulations, Mrs Joshi,' he said, smiling broadly, 'you are going to have a baby.'

I was anaemic, I had oedema, the baby's head was in the wrong position. I was advised complete bed rest. The hospital room was a familiar one. It was where I had recovered from typhoid, where Salman had materialized like a seraph and deflowered me. I was happy to be back, I felt safe, the past and the present were mixed up into a dozy continuous present. The interminable rain on the tin roof, the banks of fog that crept right into the room, the tinkle of thermometers in glasses of disinfectant, conspired to lull me into a strange sense of security.

It was when I returned to Wee Nooke that the troubles began. Although it was now autumn, the monsoon clouds had receded and the warm sun shone in a blue cloudless sky, the fog refused to go away. It crept about my forehead, black, smoky, acrid, creating a terrible weather and climate quite its own. I wept a lot, sometimes I screamed. The doctors came again. They could not understand what I was saying. I was calling out to my mother, I needed her, but she was not there. The nurses came with injections. Hiranand Headmaster looked stern and disapproving. 'You have your baby to think about, Parvati,' he said sternly, his brow knit in disapproval. 'You must try to get well.' The medicines made me sleep. I ate a lot. My body was bloated beyond recognition. Sometimes I laughed without reason.

Raju and his wife came to Nainital for their honeymoon. She had never been to the hills before. She wore a pink georgette sari, and silk ribbons in her hair. She had an expensive wristwatch and an affected smile. She looked at me with pity and concern, as though I were a sick animal or a stray dog. When Raju looked at me his face went white with shock. Guilt and repugnance battled on his face. As for me, I laughed gaily.

Masterji looked at me sternly. 'Why were you laughing like that, Parvati?' he asked me after they had left. 'What were you thinking about that was so comic?'

I started laughing again. The laughter felt good. It released me, it shook the black fog that had settled about me, like the soot on the walls in our kitchen in Jeolikote. The laughter gurgled up anew. 'It is the cosmic comedy!' I said, composing myself as much as I could.

When I went to the bathroom to wash up, I was startled by the face in the mirror. It was an old face, a fat, haggard old face; it was not my face at all. It couldn't be me, I decided. This was an imposter.

Then the sound of the water dripping from the tap, and the winter rain on the roof, and my daughter's cries as she entered the world, the ripping tearing pain of parturition; and again the dripping of the tap.

MUKUL:
DREAMS OF REASON

A LETTER FROM THE PAST

WEE NOOKE   26 February 1982
Nainital
Uttar Pradesh
India

Mukul Nainwal, Esq.
Half-Moon Apts., 17D
The Peak, Hong Kong

My dear Mukul,

By the time you receive this letter I would have expired.
I was, as you know, a nihilist. Or, should I say, an atheist. I
do not believe that I can bind you by any spiritual entreaties,
for I no longer exist.

I wish I could write and tell you what death is like. If I
get the opportunity, I certainly shall.

I was born on the last day of the last year of the last
century. The destined span of years is fast drawing to a close.

As Dr Freud has said, 'The goal of all life is Death'. I have had a lonely life.

Of all my protégés, it is to you alone that I can entrust the sum total of my Life's intellectual and material endeavours (paltry as they are) and I know you will not have pre-deceased me. Lalit is dead (poor lad!). My nephew, Pooran, is wasting himself on his newspaper. His wife is a veritable shrew. Parvati, who in her youth showed some spark of promise, is now a lunatic. Her daughter Irra is a burden on us all.

I am aware of, and can even condone, your secret vice. You were boys, Lalit and you, and it was all a long time ago. The Body, like the Heart, has its reasons. Despite all your handicaps you have made something of yourself. It is with pride that I can proclaim that I have moulded you in the image of a Gentleman. I am confident that you at least would never betray my trust.

All my life, I have unsuccessfully striven to inculcate the values of Public School Life in these hills. It was, alas, like throwing pearls before the Swines. Nainital is no longer what it once was. I cannot even bear to go down to Tallital any more, for fear of encountering some bestial ex-pupil.

As for the tourists, the less said the better. They have all but destroyed this once scenic hill station. Nainital is no different now from Meerut or Bareilly.

To come to matters of grave import, now that death is knocking at my door, I wish to settle my affairs before I depart. It is time, therefore, to convey to you the contents of my Will.

After much consideration, I have decided to leave my cottage 'Wee Nooke' with all the furniture and fittings, the orchard near Bhowali, and my library consisting of some 375 volumes to your care. It is my dearest wish, therefore, that these be put to some constructive use for the uplift of our hill folk, or for the perpetuation of my life's work, i.e., education. My solicitors, M/s R.C. Joshi and Co. (above Royal Pharmacy, Tallital), have the Deed of Will and all particulars in their custody.

You, of all my ex-students, are financially best settled, and least likely, therefore, to misappropriate my assets. Perhaps we could set up a HIRANAND JOSHI MEMORIAL TRUST. I would like to think that I have bequeathed some part of myself to posterity.

There are many who will be disappointed, even bitter, because of my decision. DO NOT let them deflect you. There is more to life than personal loss or gain. I shall depart satisfied in the knowledge that I have performed one last act of charity. It is intestinal cancer that I am dying of.

My nephew, Pooran, will, perforce, perform the last rites. But it is you, Mukul, who are my true spiritual heir.

Blessings to yourself and best regards to your wife and her child.

Affly,

Hiranand Joshi

*

The letter, forwarded to me by Messrs. R.C. Joshi & Co., rested in my pocket. The police seemed to have cleared the hold-up in the Tunnel, and the traffic crept onward, past the sodium lights of Kowloon Station to our left. Mr Myers, the auditor, was in boozy respite from the San Fransisco-Kai Tak flight. The Cantonese chauffeur had momentarily suspended his overt racial hostility to deal with the toll gate. I was unaccountably elated.

Even the faint echoes of regret, the mandatory grief, had died away by Causeway Bay.

It was with unaccustomed resolution that I had picked up the jet-lagged Mr Myers to deposit him in Furama Hotel. An unrequited love, long since forgotten, was beckoning me home.

*

That night, I dreamt of Nainital again. I dreamt that Parvati and I were swimming in the lake. We were naked. The green slimy water enveloped our newborn bodies, absolving them of lust or regret. We splashed about innocently, two children at play in a primitive paradise, until, suddenly, the waters of the lake began receding. It looked like a gurgling sink with the stopper pulled out.

The rocks under Pashan Devi lay exposed, dry and scraggy, like weeks-old chocolate cake. A ridge that ran across the water was coming into view, the hump of a disfigured dromedary. Sulphurous springs gurgled opposite Smugglers Rock. Parvati and I were standing naked on the muddy floor of the lake. Her body was as beautiful as I had always known it would be. Her breasts were not small and hard like Adeleine's, but generous and yielding. Her nipples were large and aureole, her hips ripe with the promise of infinite maternities. She was supple and sinless, and I was strong and young. But of course it was only a dream.

The next morning, I tried to explain my decision to go to Nainital to my wife, Adeleine. She listened absently, her eyes wandering, focusing now on the rubber plant in the balcony, now on the Hockney print near the window. The amah brought our coffee, and my eggs done just the way I like them.

Adeleine was displeased. Her fingers beat an angry tattoo on the ornate teak table. My wife is very good-looking in an embalmed sort of way. Her skin, once fresh as Thai orchids, feels like parchment now, and her hair is dyed raven black.

My stepdaughter, Marie, was due back from boarding school, and my English mother-in-law (my wife is Anglo-Burmese) was coming to stay. Adeleine was sceptical about my plans but I suspect she was glad to be rid of me and be alone with family.

I stumbled into marriage with Adeleine one lonely evening in Oslo. Her father was a Burmese doctor, her mother, the daughter of an English colonel, and their marriage a strange mismatch, yet another blunder, an eddy in the receding British presence in Asia.

Adeleine's first husband was a French diplomat. He had been dead only a year when I met her. She wore her husband's photograph in a gold locket on our wedding day. She mourns him still. We have no children of our own, and her daughter, Marie, now fifteen, is a little too modern for me.

I work for the International Relief Organization. Our main task is to assist the U.N. High Commission for Refugees in logistical matters. Getting leave would have been easy; we were between wars. Still, my boss, a benevolent International Civil Servant of the old school, managed to find me some affairs in Calcutta to attend to, with some consultations in New Delhi thrown in, saving me the cost of a ticket, with expenses to spare.

This relieved Adeleine somewhat, and she even packed my bags. She did not seem to grasp that Nainital is seven thousand feet above sea level, and outfitted me for a Sharjah summer. I didn't protest, so grateful was I to be able to depart. I smuggled in a coat and a cashmere cardigan from my Oslo days. Adeleine packed prodigious quantities of underwear, and five towels, and saw me to the airport. I was glad to have eluded Mr Myers and Elaine, my English mother-in-law. I felt like a schoolboy on holiday.

Hiranand Headmaster's letter nestled in my briefcase, untouched by death or grief. My youth had, at last, been bequeathed to me.

*

Uncomfortable with heights, I don't sleep well on planes. Tormented by acidity and a strange ringing in the ears, I ordered a cognac, and then another, and lulled myself into a stupor.

The stewardess awoke me as she served cryogenic orange juice to the Australian on my right. He shot the window slat up. The sun dazzled our eyes. Above the intaglio of sun, cloud and steaminess—the steaminess of the Far East, of Kowloon and Calcutta—in the far distance, through the clouds, there floated a single glittering snow peak, aloof, beckoning, majestic. I had forgotten about the Himalayas. Exhilaration swept through me.

I knew I too belonged to those exalted heights, and experienced a sudden disdain for the cattle load of tourists and executives around me. Slamming the window slat down, I dozed fitfully through the rest of the flight.

My diplomatic passport spared me the unwelcome

attentions of the customs and immigration department at Delhi.

The Delhi offices of the I.R.O. had fixed me up with a car for the journey north to Nainital. It was an air-conditioned Mercedes of doubtful vintage. The uniformed chauffeur looked like an accountant in disguise. He drove me wordlessly to Akbar Hotel. I worked off my jet lag, floundering in yet another dream that featured Adeleine, Hiranand Headmaster and Mr Myers.

I made a brief visit to our office, and met our chap there. He was a pleasant fellow, though we had nothing to discuss. I thanked him for the car, and put off the Calcutta meeting.

In the evening a colleague from my Allahabad University days who is now with the Indian government invited me home for dinner. It was raining; we sat in his veranda, and talked helplessly of politics. A winged ant sidled up my trouser leg. I remembered such insects from my college days. Neither ant nor fly, creatures of the monsoon, they live a life of brief helplessness, dead by nightfall, splattering the light bulbs with their carcasses. My mother had a theory that their day-long sojourn through earth was a karmic short cut through the obligatory 84,00,000 incarnations a human soul has to traverse.

It was a depressing evening and I was glad to leave early.

HOMEWARD BOUND

I left for Nainital before daybreak. By dawn, we had left the stifling confines of New Delhi and Ghaziabad, passing on the way what is possibly the ugliest urban architecture in the world.

We drove through Hapur, which is in every sense the perennial Indian market town. The traffic was confused, even by Hong Kong standards, and directed by an even more confused traffic policeman, who conducted the cacophony of cyclists, rickshaws, thela-walas, tongas, banana vendors and belligerent buffaloes. I noticed a puny, grotesquely sculpted figure of Ambedkar, apprehensively clutching a copy of the Indian Constitution, his other hand pointing to the closed shutters of a tandoori restaurant.

Through drought and deluge, the Indo-Gangetic plain has resisted the ministrations of its ambitious rulers. From Shah Jahan to Sanjay Gandhi, roads have been built, trees planted, canals dug. But no ruler has been able to conquer the all-encompassing tolerance of the land, nor the stubborn obedience of its people.

There was a complete familiarity in the landscape, each scene reminding me of what was coming next. The sky was like a smudged grey watercolour. My eyes followed the inky cumulonimbus cloud formations towards the most unimaginable shades of green: the young green of the paddy shoots, the deeper colours of the mango trees, the tall lush grass. There was a fulfilment in the earth, in the flooded fields and cavorting parrots, that communicated itself to me even through my tiredness of the day before. I put the window down and smelled the damp earth.

The highway was dotted with the upturned carcasses of trucks. We stopped at a level crossing. Our Mercedes effortlessly ploughed through the waiting traffic. A young boy dashed across the road, waving a ten-rupee note. A pye dog scampered after him. Vultures wheeled above like World War II planes. A man in a bullock cart joined his hands in greeting towards my car.

Every now and then we would meet a town, and pass it, and return to the fields of green waving paddy. At Garhmukteshwar we came upon the Ganga, distended by the monsoons. The driver asked to stop for tea, but I told him we would halt at Moradabad.

As we crossed the river, the sun glinted on its yellow-brown waves. They were a strange colour, like the eyes of someone I could not remember but knew I did not trust. I thought of Hiranand Headmaster, whose ashes must have meandered past here beneath me. His death, and mine with it, and mortality itself, suddenly crowded the car. I am not comfortable with such thoughts, I have a rule about never contemplating death, so I willed myself to sleep. The steady progress of the car soothed me.

Moradabad woke me up even before the driver did. He asked if I wanted a cup of tea. I eyed the dhaba where we had halted. O.K. Café did not look in the least OK. I am not a fastidious man, but the surroundings discouraged me. Moradabad had not changed.

I knew the city well from my stint in the Indian Administrative Service. It had been famous for '*machhar, makkhi aur Mussalman*'; it was evident that this was still the case. It was a Victorian industrial nightmare, an urban disaster, a punishment posting for us civil servants. It was here, in a government bungalow that rejoiced in the name of 'Cedars', that I had first encountered that strange folding contraption, a Collector's chair. It was here that I once swallowed a fly in my beer, here that I ran into a cow and almost provoked a riot.

I had no pleasant memories of Moradabad. The grit and the grime and the locomotive soot, the sultry heat and the sounds of trucks, trains and cycle rickshaws, were all encroaching into the uncertain sanctuary of the parked car in which I sat. The spectral circles reflecting upon the petrol spills on the puddles by the roadside provided the only beauty in sight.

I looked for the driver. He was sitting by the dhaba, holding his tea glass with a handkerchief, staring at me. There was a hint of amusement in his eyes. But amusement at what? Could he be mocking me? I felt oddly threatened. I am vulnerable to ridicule, and, in a certain light, he looked disconcertingly like Mr Myers.

I distracted myself with a favourite pastime. If I were famous, and someone asked me to list my eight favourite composers, what would I reply? I am no musicologist, but I know what I like. The answers flashed in my mind as though in a TV quiz.

1. Bach
2. Mozart
3. Brahms
4. Beethoven

My mind blocked. I could not summon another name, not recall a single score or composition. The insistent ugliness of my surroundings had possessed me. Ravi Shankar? But was he a composer? Not exactly, I decided, as the driver returned and we set off again.

We passed sugar-factory smells, and through the stubbly fields of cane I could see track-mounted cane trolleys hauled by magisterial elephants.

Soon, we were in Rampur, where the plundering Rohilla tribes had once established an ephemeral cultural capital. Rampur had been the home town of the poet Hasrat Rampuri. I was overtaken by nostalgia and remembrance. The driver asked if I wanted a wash. 'But where can we stop?' I enquired irritably. 'I hate railway stations.'

'At the Palace,' he replied cryptically. Without waiting for my reply he turned the car to the left, off the main road and into the township. Soon, a grotesque hand-painted sign in a stylized mock-Persian English script advertised that we were approaching the vicinity of the Palace Guest-House-cum-Coffee Shoppe.

The Mercedes slithered into the portico of a derelict building of palatial proportions. An old man, dressed in white Aligarhi trousers and a short kurta, with an elegantly trimmed white beard, rushed down the steps to welcome us. He was so effusive in his greetings that I thought at first he had mistaken me for someone he knew. He ushered me into a large durbar hall, and broke the dimness of the room by switching on two asymmetrically placed fluorescent lights. The walls were painted an Islamic green. Four cheap Rexine sofas were arranged across the marble floor, and odd-sized tables stood before them, each holding a steel jug and a typed menu. There was no one else in the room.

The old man's Urdu was so fluent and mellifluous that I surrendered myself to the flow of his conversation. He got me a pot of coffee and some toast, and stationed himself deferentially behind my sofa, from where he unleashed a melancholy lament upon the decay of the state.

'The poet Hasrat Rampuri was a friend of mine,' I said casually, as he swept the persistent flies off the open jam jar on my table. He did not seem as pleased as I had anticipated. In fact he responded with an abrupt cessation of hospitality.

'Would you like to use the toilet?' he asked coldly, and led me to the damp ineffective closet near the door. When I returned to my table he was nowhere to be seen. I prowled around the abandoned rooms in search of him and came upon a deserted courtyard which led to a further maze of empty rooms. Another old man was seated by the side of a broken fountain fashioned like a crescent moon.

'You can't go any further,' the second old man said, his broken teeth garbling the words. 'It was forbidden for strangers to enter the harem.'

I retraced my steps with some difficulty, only to find the first old man standing by the Mercedes chatting to the driver. He seemed offended with me still.

'What about the bill?' I asked hesitantly, uncertain of the nature of my gaffe.

'Consider, my son, that you have partaken of my hospitality,' he said haughtily, as with a swift, formal bow he strode back into the palace.

I pondered the mystery in the car, looking out into the rain. Whatever could have offended him? I had evidently touched a raw nerve. But then Hasrat had never been an entirely likeable man.

Hasrat Rampuri had been the head of the department of English in the Allahabad University when I studied there. The undisputed doyen of Urdu poetry, toothless, venerable, dressed always in the same brown khadi jacket with dal stains on it, he became the object of my instant and total idolatry.

It was at a mushaira that I had first observed him, in the same dal-stained jacket, lolling on the stage, sipping mischievously from a brown earthen teacup.

'What are you drinking, Hasrat Mia?' somebody in the audience had asked. Hasrat had run his hands through his greying hair, a true poetic gesture, a stance, almost. 'It's milk, mother's milk, from Parnassus,' he had replied, his eyes bloodshot, his tongue faltering. I was charmed.

That same evening, after the mushaira, I got into an argument with a lecturer from Farrukhabad. 'Urdu is nothing but a decadent and obsolete language,' I told him. I was trying to be clever, but he was from Farrukhabad, and doubled a fist at my front teeth, and now, many years later, despite the attentions of many diligent dentists, they are still crooked and vulnerable.

We left the outskirts of Rampur. The sky darkened, the rain intensified. I remembered Hasrat's pale eyes, grey and exultant, as at a seminar when he would explain the concept of 'Meghdoot' to us. I, too, could imagine the poet Kalidasa exhorting these soaring monsoon clouds, as they travelled from the teardrop of Sri Lanka up this beloved triangular subcontinent, only to be rebuffed by my Himalayas.

Then, of course, there is Eliot. What the thunder said. Da. Da. Da.

I listened to the rain, and the strains of Raga Megh Malhar cascaded through my consciousness. I pondered this journey, this path, which I had travelled so many times before, so very long ago.

Every landmark had a corresponding echo in my memories. Here I had passed, at fourteen, on my first visit to the plains, full of hope. And then, heartbroken after her marriage, I had travelled this same dusty road, in my new official jeep, to meet Parvati and her husband Lalit in Bareilly. I had needed desperately to show off, to display my success, to inform her about the wrong decision she had made.

Lalit was dead now, and Parvati insane. I had loved them both. These were not passing memories, nor were they daydreams. Older and wiser, I was at last returning home.

I was fated however to soon encounter an implausible trio of fellow-travellers, who took the edge off my romantic musings for a while.

TRAVELLER'S TALES

We arrive now at the strange tale of Rakesh Kumar, purveyor of carburettors, his friend the restaurateur Ramlala and their flatulent sidekick Prithipal Singh, origins unknown.

'Myself Rakesh Kumar,' the archetypal fool's face announced as it thrust itself into the interior of my car.

The driver had ventured out into the flooded fields to relieve himself. It would have made an interesting photograph. I was musing upon the composition when I was interrupted by a sound closer onomatopoeically to a rat-a-tat-tat than any sound I have heard before or since.

Rat-a-tat-tat, he knocked, rat-a-tat-tat. Surprised, I opened the door. Forked lightning stood mirrored in his eyes. Thunder drowned his words. I shut the door again.

It was a vacant face, acne scarred, in which only the lips were set in an expressive 'O' of perpetual astonishment. As I stared back in disbelief, a long arm prised open the door of the car. A man sidled in and settled himself beside me.

Two more faces materialized and peered in imploringly.

The first man began telling me the story of his life.

'Myself, Rakesh Kumar,' he began, 'and these gentlemen outside, Ramlala and Prithipal Singh.' Concealing my bewilderment, I allowed him to continue.

'If I may modestly state, myself being the resident of Meerut, this morning set out on this journey full of hope. But, alas! Uneasy lies the head that wears the crown! For I am, of date, a ruined man!'

I could make no sense of this strange introduction, but he carried on regardless. There was something compelling about his frenetic monologue.

'I set off for Nainital this morning,' he continued in an adenoidal wheeze. 'For pleasure and joy of walking and to pay deposit for a shop. My sister-in-law is wishing to open showroom there, a Vimal textiles showroom. At Moradabad, I was under a tree, chewing paan. You understand paan? Yes, betel leaf. As I was thus chewing, and discussing with Prithipal Singh, as I was thus engaged in time passing, my bus departed for the hilly place. And, Sir Ji, with her, seated within, my sum total of life savings, fifteen thousand bucks! In a white-and-blue bag of the Pan Am Airlines! Now Sir Ji, sea is in Nainital!'

Taken aback by the flow of his rhetoric, I could only protest that there was no sea in Nainital, but a lake, a lake. He started back uncomprehendingly. I perceived through the corner of my eye that Prithipal Singh had taken the opportunity to seat himself in the car with us.

The driver returned, and started the car. 'Don't ignite!' Rakesh Kumar screeched, his eyeballs orbs of depthless horror. Prithipal Singh thrust the door open. Now Ramlala scrambled in, leaving muddy puddles about him, and shaking the water off his clothes in a markedly canine fashion.

The panic subsided. Rakesh Kumar extracted a soggy cigarette from the pocket of his damp sky-blue safari suit. Flicking it with an expert movement into the waiting circlet of his mouth, he resumed the conversation. 'Sea is in Nainital,' he said fervently, 'and I must follow suit.'

Hill people, and especially residents of eastern UP, habitually confuse the use of the hard and the soft 'S'. 'Sea', who ever she was, seemed to be in the hills, as were Rakesh Kumar's life savings. I caught the driver's laughing eyes reflected in the rear-view mirror, but this time I knew whom he was mocking, and smiled back.

'Sir Ji, I fall at your feets,' Rakesh Kumar exclaimed, matching the action to his words. 'Please permit me and these illiterates to ride in your car in chase of my wealth!'

Far be it from my intentions to sneer at a fellow-human's abuse of what was, after all, to him a foreign tongue. Yet I must confess my horror at the prospect of re-entering the sacred repository of my childhood in the company of quite such a Sancho Panza. I did not know, however, quite how to articulate my protest, which was, as I chided myself, essentially social.

And so we set off together in search of our separate grails. Prithipal Singh pointed to his podgy feet and announced glumly that he had on only one rubber chappal, having dropped the other in the excitement of getting Ramlala into the car.

'Arrey, doesn't matter, yaar, I will buy you many more,' Rakesh Kumar said munificently. His spirits seemed to have revived. I watched bemused as he wriggled and squirmed beside me before finally extracting a soggy matchbox from the pocket of his trousers. He couldn't, despite his best efforts, ignite it.

It was bad enough to be thus sandwiched between two cretins in my official Mercedes. It was, however, as we were approaching the hills that the problem began. I don't quite know how to put this in polite language, but subsequently a foul smell wafted through the car, preceded by an impressive and unmistakable percussion from Prithipal Singh's posterior.

Rakesh Kumar smiled appeasingly. 'I only met him at Moradabad,' he said defensively, 'where he joined in my hot chase.'

It transpired that Rakesh Kumar had boarded the bus to Nainital in Meerut, with his cash bag. At the rest stop in Moradabad, he had lounged about too long and too late. The bus, the mystical 'sea', departed for Nainital, and Rakesh Kumar's Pan Am bag and his life savings of fifteen thousand bucks with her.

Ramlala was the fruit-juice-wala to whom Rakesh Kumar had rushed for counsel upon the discovery of his financial loss. Inexplicably, Ramlala had shut his stall and joined in the chase. Together, they shanghaied Prithipal Singh and clambered on to a truck in pursuit of the perfidious bus, only to be abandoned near Bilaspur for unspecified reasons. I suspected that Prithipal Singh, God's warning against gastric excess, could well have been the cause.

'And where from your good self arrives, Sir Ji?' Rakesh Kumar asked, still smiling that unbearable ingratiating smile which had already failed to endear him to me.

'Hong Kong.'

'Hong Kong?' he responded incredulously.

'I just flew in yesterday,' I said world-wearily, my mood softening.

'I should have known it!' he exclaimed, and then, for the edification of the company, 'Hong Kong is a colony of the USA.'

'The British actually, and it reverts back to China soon.' I said apologetically, for I have a passion for fact.

'I love Chinese,' he continued grandly, 'Chinese food and Chinese fun.' He winked and gave me a meaningful nudge. Prithipal Singh broke wind again. A sense of nightmare began engulfing me.

I could see the faint shadow of the hills, like a woman's moustache. To insulate myself, I began daydreaming. If I were famous, and an interviewer were to ask me to list my five favourite authors, what would I reply?

1. Rushdie, undoubtedly, Salman Rushdie
2. Gabriel Garcia Marquez
3. V.S. Naipaul (a bit dry)
4. Pablo Neruda
5. Graham Greene

We stopped at the petrol station in Kathgodam. The hills were before us. I got off. My journey, I felt, had only now truly begun. The air was clear and silent. Monkeys chattered on a stone parapet. Alongside a map of the lake district of Kumaon, a rusty billboard announced the pleasures of Nainital. It pictured brightly coloured yachts with striped sails, and women in sleeveless blouses sipping cola drinks as they watched the ducks.

Rakesh Kumar loped to the board and pointed towards the blue of Nainital on the map, where his fifteen thousand rupees, or their absence, awaited him. The nail of his little finger was grotesquely long. It had been carefully filed and was painted a gleaming red colour. He directed it at a blue arrow which announced, 'YOU ARE HERE.'

The trio resettled themselves into the car. I stifled an ineffectual protest, and watched helplessly as Ramlala ensconced himself in front beside the driver, leaving me seated stiffly between Rakesh Kumar and Prithipal Singh.

We began the winding journey up, through the lower Shivaliks and the sub-Himalayan ranges into the forests of tall sal trees, and still higher to the gaunt coniferous slopes.

I fumbled for my cashmere sweater, which lay folded in a bag beside the chauffeur. Ramlala looked at it longingly. I suspected that he was already regretting his impulse to adventure.

The driver halted at Jeolikote to replenish the radiator of the car. Fresh spring water gurgled from a lion-headed spout. I sniffed the cool aroma of rain-soaked mud. A fair, even-featured young boy came up selling roasted corn. Nostalgia overcame me. I couldn't resist buying five cobs, one for each of us.

We stopped next at the toll station outside Nainital. Huge heads of dahlias nodded in the breeze. There were marigolds and cosmos and tiger lilies and other sorts of hill flowers the names of which I did not know. Monsoon streams gurgled down the hillside. Butterflies speckled the air.

'Where every prospect pleases, and only man is vile,' I murmured to myself. Rakesh Kumar and Prithipal Singh were lolling as though in a stupor on either side of me, the remnants of the corn spattered about them. I was eyeing them with distaste when suddenly Ramlala vaulted out the front seat towards a parked yellow-and-blue Kumaon

Roadways bus. The chauffeur leapt out as well to follow him and a split second later Rakesh Kumar and Prithipal Singh were galloping behind them.

I was left to cope with the old man in ancient bifocal spectacles who shuffled forward to collect the toll.

'How many in the car?' he asked, peering in as if to check for any truants hiding beneath the seats.

'Five of us' I replied in Pahari. He stared suspiciously at me. His eyes said, you may know the language but you are just a rich tourist. I felt rebuffed.

I was still nursing my rejection when suddenly the doors of the car were flung open, and Rakesh Kumar was all over me, hugging me and planting wet circlets of affection upon my cheeks. As I struggled to release myself, he thrust the blue-and-white Pan Am bag before my eyes, then unzipped it open with a flourish and extracted wads and wads of soiled hundred-rupee notes, which he waved about him in an exultant fan dance. His companions stared at him as though mesmerized. Their eyes were ablaze with a vicarious financial lust.

One-slippered Prithipal Singh was despatched to the Khumcha to buy tea and biscuits for us all. As I sipped at the sweet hot brew, I said proprietorially, 'At least we hill people are honest. You have to grant us that. Where else would anyone return fifteen thousand rupees to a...(Cretin?) (Ass?)'

As I was fumbling for the polite phrase, a sly bulb of contempt lit up in Rakesh Kumar's eyes. 'Honest?' he exclaimed. 'Honest? Or fool? You tell me that, Sir Ji! You tell me that! After all it was myself I who took this great business ricks!' Spittle dripped from the side of his mouth as he sprayed his views at me full face.

I was speechless with rage. Before I could respond, he enveloped me in another malodorous hug, and presented me with his visiting card, insisting that I deposit it safely in my wallet. He took mine in exchange, and promised to stay with me if ever he came to Hong Kong, as he certainly would now that he had a friend there.

A small crowd had gathered outside, eager for a glimpse of the man who had thus jousted with fate and won. Rakesh Kumar was strangely at ease in the role of a folk hero, and seemed already to have forgotten his comrades in distress. He shook hands with me again, and disappeared in a haze of glory, followed by his two hopeful sidekicks, never to be seen again, or so I presumed at that moment.

FIRST ENCOUNTERS

I arrived at Nainital. It was changed, changed utterly. The buildings were all in a state of incredible dilapidation. Everywhere, people swarmed like flies as though the entire population of the district were present at Tallital upon my arrival. Tourists, porters, guides and coolies engulfed our car.

Beyond their jostling figures and bobbing heads lay the lake. The mid-afternoon sun reflected gently off its rippling surface. I looked at it for a long time. A pool of loneliness that had been travelling within me slid gratefully into the tranquil waters. I felt I was finally home, never again to wander or stray into the troubled world below.

The driver masterfully dismissed the porters and hotel agents, and deposited me safely at Relax Inn, where the Delhi office of the I.R.O. had thoughtfully made a reservation. I refused the offer of a late lunch, and slept off my accumulated travel weariness.

Some hours later, reclining on a wicker chair in the veranda of Relax Inn, I contemplated the quiet translucent rainless evening, and munched the soggy biscuits that had been set on a plate before me. A soft grey-pink haze sat upon the pebbled garden. The air was filled with the melancholy chirping of crickets and the distant laughter of children. Somewhere, an invisible flautist was playing a mountain air. From the lily pond in the garden came the occasional liquid splosh of a fish breaking the surface. A dog yelped excitedly.

The thin mist was creeping about the quiet garden. It was getting chilly. There had been no homecoming. Perhaps there was no home for me to come to, here, or anywhere else.

Hiranand Headmaster's disinherited family had all trooped in within half an hour of my arrival, for the small-town tom-tom is as efficient as it is unsparing. His nephew, Pooran, had arrived with his wife Neera, their two sons, and, a little distance behind, as befitting her dependent status, Parvati's daughter Irra.

We had sat here, in the veranda, listening to the plops and splashes from the fish pond. Irra was almost as old as Parvati had been when I had first known her. She was dressed in a blue salwar-kameez with a white chunni. The uniform was heartrendingly familiar, for Parvati too had attended the Government Girls Inter College. When we were young it had been a great joke between Lalit and myself to ask her where she studied.

'GGIC, Ji,' Parvati would invariably reply. This would provoke us to uncontrollable mirth, and we would laugh until our stomachs ached. 'GGIC, Ji!' we would mimic. 'Ha! Ha! Ha!'

I couldn't help myself. 'Where do you study?' I had asked Irra gently.

'GGIC, Ji,' she replied demurely. A great deal of understanding had passed between us in those few words.

'I'm very tired today,' I told Pooran. 'I'll come and visit you at Wee Nooke tomorrow.' I had shooed them off and returned to my musings.

Hiranand Headmaster's letters had been in the nature of scientific and sociological minutiae interspersed with philosophical asides, and much whining about his health. His scrawling handwritten missives had left me quite unprepared for the shock of once again encountering Parvati's limpid eyes in her young daughter's face.

I wondered about Irra's name. I could only connect it with the river Irrawady, in Burma, which reminded me of my wife, for whom I had not spared a thought since leaving Hong Kong. Adeleine and Nainital? The two were quite incompatible, I told myself guiltlessly.

My thoughts returned to Irra, and her mother Parvati, whom I had once loved to distraction. Parvati had rejected me because I am not a Thuldhoti Brahmin like herself and had, instead, married my best friend Lalit Joshi at Hiranand Headmaster's behest.

Lalit was long dead and Parvati confined to the mental asylum in Bareilly. That was how hope and beauty usually ended here in our hills.

The evening had darkened into night, and I was still sitting on the veranda. I could hear doors and windows being noisily shut. Someone switched the veranda light on, but still I sat dreaming of Parvati, and her daughter who should have been mine.

I have a stepdaughter, Marie. She and I are scarcely on the best of terms. She is a brittle modern creature, unburdened by any sorrow. I thought of Irra, and her soft sad eyes that had seemed to plead with me. Chiding myself for sentimentality, I buttoned my cardigan and went in.

Relax Inn is managed by three middle-aged brothers, all bachelors, all bearded, and frankly speaking, all rather boring. The youngest, Jeewan, had been with me in school, where he had once suffered an attack of jaundice. The sobriquet was thereupon conferred upon him, for nicknames are popular in Kumaon, and he was known for ever after as Jeewan Jaundice. This served to distinguish him from Jeewan Jalebi or any other Jeewans that might crop up.

Jeewan Jaundice was already at the dining table with his brothers, Sohan Selfish and Mohan Mischief. I sat down with them and allowed myself to be lauded as the local boy who had made good. Naturally, they knew all about my circumstances and the purpose of my visit to Nainital. Apparently the state government was planning to build a ropeway to Snow View. Jeewan J. assured me that this would render Wee Nooke a most accessible and lucrative piece of real estate. The three brothers were themselves quite keen to purchase the property, and convert it into a tourist camp. Of course this was impossible under the terms of the will.

'We want to expand, to increase our capacity,' Sohan Selfish explained. 'We are beginning to get a lot of foreigners off season.' He told me of Japanese and Finns and birdwatchers and American families who came at Christmas, until I began to feel this was not Nainital but Macao.

Having thus established their prosperity and contentment, the three abandoned themselves to an involved session of slander, suggestion and innuendo. I was an outsider apropos the local gossip, but I could still salvage many familiar names, and found myself ascertaining whether Neeta was Meena's daughter, and if Basant had fulfilled the promise of his youth, and did they remember Navin, whose father had owned a car?

'Our Jeewan had wanted to marry Basant's sister,' Mohan Mischief said suddenly. Jeewan looked wistful and embarrassed.

'Why didn't he?' I asked tactlessly.

'Ija wouldn't let him,' Mohan replied, laughing a strange pointless laugh. 'She wouldn't let him. You know what mothers are like.'

'I know,' I replied. I had been abroad when my mother died. I did not attend her funeral. I would have been ashamed to introduce my mother to Adeleine or to my English mother-in-law Elaine.

'Our Ija wants us to get married first,' Mohan said self importantly. 'She wants me and Sohan to bring wives home. But we want her to choose, because, after all, we can trust her choice.'

'Women,' Sohan Selfish said, relishing the word. 'You have to be careful when you choose a woman.'

'I wouldn't want a bossy woman,' Mohan said speculatively. 'After all, a man is the head of the family. That's why I want my mother to choose a wife for me. She knows about women.'

'You had always wanted to marry Hiranandji's niece Parvati, didn't you, Mukul?' Jeewan asked, exchanging hurt for hurt.

'That was a long time ago,' I said tonelessly.

'Well, it's all turned out for the best, except for Parvati,' Sohan said, with an inappropriate degree of relief.

I changed the subject. The brothers were still at their chicken curry.

The grandfather clock in the hall struck ten. It had been purchased wholesale with all the other Victorian memorabilia from the Swiss memsahib who had presided over the establishment in the days of the British Raj, when Relax Inn had still been Relax Inn. The stern chimes of the clock echoed through the entire incongruous ambience of the room; the stiff chairs, the Chinese screens, the faded watercolours of dead European women, the gilded mirrors. It pertained to another world entirely, the world to which I had once aspired and to which I now belonged, but without conviction.

I suffered a sudden crisis of identity, and turned in a sort of panic to the three brothers. They were solid and reassuring. They had contributed the plastic flowers to the vases, the scenic wallpaper to the lounge. They entertained no doubts about who they were.

I closed my eyes. Adeleine's face materialized like an obedient genie. 'Calm down,' I could hear her whisper, 'count to ten. Don't overreact.'

I shut my eyes tighter, and counted to ten. When I opened them again the three brothers were all trooping out of the room.

'It's time to say goodnight to Ija,' Mohan Mischief said. I fell into line with them as they crowded into the little room beside the landing where their mother lived.

Their mother was the oldest woman I had seen for a very long time. She had dull silver hair and a pale, freckled skin. She was dressed in a cream cotton sari and a woollen shawl, and lay on a low bed, her mottled hands extruding from the bleached mull coverlet on the quilt. Faded colourless eyes peered inquisitively from behind black-framed spectacles.

All around her, brilliantly coloured pictures of gods and goddesses emblazoned the walls. Rama and Sita jostled with Krishna. There was a calendar of Lord Shiva at his meditations, entwined with serpents, and the Ganga spouting fitfully from his locks. An outdated calendar had Parvati, or at least I assumed it was her, plucking flowers from a celestial garden, surrounded by handmaidens.

On the floor near Ija's bed was a small wooden mandir, like a doll's house. It sheltered a Shiva linga, a Ganesh and several other deities. Before it rested a brown cloth-bound *Ramcharitmanas*, a conch shell, a brass prayer bell with a carved Nandi bull upon its handle and an aarti. Fruits and flowers were piled on a plate. A damp, musky smell hung about the room, the smell of incense and shut windows and old age.

Ija was still staring at me. She sat up energetically, mouthing a loud toothless gabble. Her breasts were exposed under the woollen shawl. I stared in fascination at the pale withered dugs as Jeewan gently lay her down. 'Go to sleep now, Ija,' he said softly, and we tiptoed out.

THE SISTERS OF EVE

The three brothers were engaged in a whispered conversation by the landing. 'What nonsense! Of course I'm not afraid of the daayan,' I overheard Mohan Mischief say, 'It's just that I don't feel like going out alone.'

Dim fearful memories stirred in my mind. 'Did you mention a daayan?' I asked him astonishedly. 'I always thought a daayan was a witch!'

'Yes,' Sohan Selfish replied informatively, 'A daayan is a witch with inverted feet.'

'You know how Nainital loves gossip and exaggeration,' Jeewan whispered, his voice trembling. 'There's a big scare about one prowling around these day. Ghouls and familiars everywhere! Mohan daju was scared to go along to the Nandashtami fair. We were only teasing him for being afraid.'

'I never realized that the Nandashtami mela would be on these days,' I said, 'Dussehra must be approaching.'

'I still don't want to go alone,' Mohan Mischief said mulishly. Sohan proceeded upstairs, insisting that he was too old and tired to attend village fairs.

'Are the two of you tired as well, then? Or are you afraid the daayan might pounce upon you?' Mohan said, laughing a silly cackling laugh, his crooked teeth and slightly squint eyes giving him a wild look.

'No daayan would ever pounce upon us,' Jeewan said wistfully. He was tall, bearded, balding. He had mild eyes and a certain Germanic bearing.

'Did you know that Jeewan daju began shaving at twenty-two? He was as hairless as a young girl until then.' Mohan cackled.

I recalled this as being factually correct, and looked with new respect at his Tolstoyan growth.

We set off for the mela, talking all the way of daayans and twals and other mountain familiars. The asphalt road winds down some impossible curves before it arrives at the flats. The flats are not flats as found in town or city, although there are plenty of those coming up in Nainital now, but the local name given to the flattened stretch of ground at the Mallital end of the lake, formed by the rubble of the great landslide of 1880.

Birch leaves shuddered in the wind. Strange shadows played with the scattered lamp posts, grey creeping on grey. Our elongated shadows performed a slow eerie dance. The moon lay hidden behind clouds that glimmered with a yellowish excitable light.

We walked past the old English graveyard of St. Johns-in-the-Wilderness, with its brooding trees, with roots like talons, past the stables where horses sheltered restlessly under tattered blankets, down past the mosque and the police station to the temple. There is another shorter way, across the parking lot, but Jeewan had wanted to buy cigarettes.

The comforting glow of lights from the temple decorations came into view. Rows upon rows of coloured bulbs were strung radially into an incandescent tent. Even the gurdwara was gaily illuminated. Many of the shops were already half shut. Their owners lay dozing inside. Shawls and bangles and ribbons were hung in confused colourful display. Sticky looking jalebis and other sweetmeats were piled in unappetizing heaps beside enormous frying pots.

Everybody appeared possessed by a reckless abandoned gaiety. A well dressed old man was walking a pet monkey on a chain. I heard the crashing of cymbals and the merry sound of a tambourine, followed by the arrival of a young man dressed as a woman. He was swaying sensuously to the music, his lean hips looking strangely attractive under the billowing skirts. I felt a momentary tremor of sexual excitement, which I quelled with a stern rebuke.

The night was cold and the ground damp with monsoon sludge. We stopped at a shooting gallery with coloured balloons where local youths were swaggering about with a Daisy gun. Straggling revellers were grouped around an almost empty Ferris wheel. College boys loped around in groups of threes and fours, their arms linked about each other's shoulders. There was scarcely a woman to be seen, save a plump excited matron clutching at her sari, as the chill wind whistled through the flats.

A young Tibetan woman was sitting alone at a stall near the temple, quite indifferent to her surroundings. Dressed in a long black baku, she was half reclining upon a battered tin trunk, her wares spread out on the ground before her. Her slanting Mongolian eyes were heavily made up, their clear almond shape emphasized by the thick eyeliner.

I was intrigued, and found myself walking over to examine the tiny scent bottles and heavily-set stone jewellery with exaggerated interest. The Tibetan girl pointed to a small ivory scent bottle. It was prettily carved, but did not have a stopper.

Staring at her fine brown hands I shuddered with a convulsion of physical lust such as I had never felt before. I wanted very much to touch her hands, and I did. They felt like dry leaves. She said nothing, made no response save to stare silently back.

Mohan and Jeewan caught up with me, and we hurried into the temple. Walking beneath the three arched gates I remembered so well from my childhood, I was transported into the past. I became again a boy of eleven, clutching at my mother's blouse, as we picked our way across mutilated leprous beggars down the seven steps to the vast vermilion figure of Hanuman. Here I had used to plead to his impassive simian countenance for courage and protection from lurking shadows on the way home.

I was so wrapped up in the past that I forgot to even take off my shoes, and the brothers had to remind me. Jeewan got me a ticket for their storage, a temporary measure, he explained, to deal with the crowds during the mela.

Inside the temple courtyard drunken young men with transistor radios slung around their shoulders were dancing in ragged circles. They were treading with slow deliberate steps, their arms linked together, singing sad-sounding, wailing songs.

'*Lalli ho, Lalli ho Lalla,*' they hummed, their bodies surrendered to the movement and the music.

A man lay on the wet ground as though convulsed by a seizure. He was whimpering softly to himself. Occasionally he would slouch to a sitting position and articulate faint cries and screams, which, Mohan informed me, were prophesies regarding the future of India. I disdain superstition, although I suppose it has its place in every society, and left the two brothers to witness what was in all probability nothing more or less than an epileptic stroke.

I had the sensation of somehow being incorporated into a painting by Heironimus Bosch. Determined not to lose myself in the mass emotions around me, I decided to inspect the twin images of Nanda and Sunanda, the tutelary goddesses of our hills.

A havan was being conducted by an old priest dressed in a dhoti and a balaclava. The stern images of the two goddesses stood vigil over the calm faces of the Pahari women, seated cross-legged before the timid flames of the sacred fire, proud and serene in their festival finery.

The oddly dressed priest was holding an enormous microphone in one hand. The sound of his prayers echoed across the mountains. There was a lot of feedback from the loudspeakers, but somehow it only added to the resonance of his recitation. As I listened to the sonorous beauty of his voice, and watched the quiet Pahari women, tranquil, self-possessed, and quite oblivious to the noise and revelry about them, I felt strangely moved. Something about the moment, some half-remembered accumulation of passionate experience, suddenly evoked, nearly choked me.

The half-moon was peering through the clouds, and through the corner of my eye I could see a frisky young lamb being led trustingly to slaughter.

The wind had become a gentle whisper, stirring the leaves of quiescent trees, lighting their patient rugged barks as it shook the rows of circularly strung bulbs. A temple bell chimed softly in the breeze. Its sound was distinct from all the other sounds, from the revelry of the fairground, the filmy music of the bioscope, the steady incantation of the priest, the crackle of the microphone, the murmur of the wind. It was separate and yet it was integral to the whole.

I discovered that I was weeping. The tears streaming silently down my cheeks turned to unaccountable heaving sobs as I fell prostrate upon the steps of the first of the four inner shrines. Although the doors were locked, I knew that it was the temple of Naina Devi, of the Goddess Parvati whose husband is Shiva. Her eyes had become the verdant lake whose peaceful waters even now murmured behind us. My mother, my home, forgive and bless and regenerate, I wept.

A great calm upon me, I dried my tears and walked smiling towards the steps facing the lake, Mohan and Jeewan sauntering behind like shadows. I groped my way down until I reached the bottom step where the lake, swollen by the monsoon, lapped gently at the slime-coated cement near my feet. The lake looked black and mysterious. The street lights dissolved and reflected upon its shores. A few rowboats were tethered by thick ropes to the iron clamps on the steps. They bobbed gently in the dark.

The brothers had seated themselves a few steps above me. I sat absolutely still, digesting my exaltation, jealous to disturb or share it. Mohan clambered down beside me, in the looming shadow of the temple, and lit a cigarette. The acrid sweet smell of marijuana wafted towards me. I looked at him questioningly. Misunderstanding my glance, he offered me the cigarette. In the same spirit of exaltation, I partook of a few careless puffs, and was immediately sorry for my action. I began feeling very strange indeed. I think I told them I was leaving, and floated off, nodding obeisance to the devi as I left. I couldn't locate my shoes, and walked off in the first pair I could find, up the hill, back towards the hotel.

Although as a child I lived in Tallital, I often used to walk this way to visit my cousin Milind who had lived near Sleepy Hollow. There was a bend, just above Metropole Hotel, that used to inexplicably terrify me, and I discovered that the terror still remained. I could not define it, but there was a brooding threat in the landscape, the genius loci was somehow not benevolent.

I found I was afraid, and glanced involuntarily over my shoulder. My shadow, dwarfed and diminished, turned as well. Of course there was nobody, but from behind the curve of the hill I could hear the sound of anklets, delicately jingling to a steady tread, approaching me. Chhink chhink, they tinkled, chhink chhink, louder now, accompanied by a reedy feminine voice humming an unknown tune.

The road curved again. I glanced behind me fearfully, and stood still, waiting, sweating, transfixed, as a slim figure, sheathed from head to toe in a black burqa, approached me. Only her hands were visible, her hands and her eyes, and these only dimly, for the street lights were few and far between. The fingernails were hennaed orange. They fluttered like pale moths.

'Why are you staring, haven't you seen a woman before?' she asked laughingly, waving those pale hands in arch rhythm to her question. She was wearing a cheap digital watch. Her voice was musical and cultured, but the laugh was theatrical, hysterical even.

I could only continue to stare, and so we stood, for a few seconds, until Mohan and Jeewan lumbered into view, and I rushed in relief towards them.

She looked at us provocatively for a moment. 'Scared, are you? I'm not from the Lal Tanki, you know,' she taunted, in that bright mocking voice. She flounced her head, and turned back in the direction she had come from, still laughing that weird theatrical laugh, which echoed even after she had disappeared around the curve of the hill.

I fell into step with the others. 'Do you think that was the daayan?' Jeewan asked tremulously after we had walked in silence for a while. 'Did you notice her feet?'

'I didn't notice, she was in a burqa,' I said helplessly.

Mohan made a lewd remark which cleared the air. We walked companionably home, Mohan daju whistling an aimless tune, and Jeewan lighting the darker, rockier bits with his pocket torch.

PILGRIM'S PROGRESS

The next morning I awoke as though for the first time. My sinuses were clear, my head was light, my responses quite unburdened by the weight of forty-seven years. The patch of sky visible from the window was brilliant and unclouded. A bluebottle sat buzzing on the windowpane, trapped between the wire mesh and the white voile blinds.

My room was directly above the downstairs veranda, and overlooked the garden. It was furnished with two cots with foam mattresses. An overpolished dressing table held a small paraffin lamp and some candles. Several rugs and dhurries were layered on the floor, one over the other, to disguise the tears and bare patches. There was a doubtful looking wardrobe, a table, a standard lamp, an ashtray, and a pristine copy of Gideons Bible.

The adjoining bathroom was white-tiled and quite hygienic. I bathed and dressed. Folding my pyjamas, I consigned them to the cavernous wardrobe and walked past a dozen unoccupied rooms to the dining room downstairs, ready for my morning coffee.

At that unlikely hour, I found Sohan, Mohan and Jeewan kneading their way through mountains of pungent-smelling dal bhat. I have always considered the lack of cutlery or of any form of gastronomic implement in my homeland to betray a distressing culinary barbarism. Even the Chinese use chopsticks. I averted my eyes from the glutinous mess that was drying and cracking on their fingers, and from the little border of dal rimming Mohan's moustache. Checking my revulsion, I settled myself resolutely opposite them.

'You should be hurrying, Pooran Paper will be waiting for you,' Mohan Mischief said.

Jeewan rose to my defence 'Let him sleep late, he's on holiday,' he said protectively. Without consulting me he ordered the waiter (also with yellow dal stains on his grimy jacket) to bring me a thali.

Like Proust and his madeleines, the heaped plate before me evoked the entire gamut of motivations that had persuaded me to leave the hills. It signified poverty, necessity and monotony. It was connected in my mind with the cows we had kept, and my mother who always smelt of dal, milk and cow dung. Or perhaps it was just that my mother had always been a very bad cook. I could still remember the taste and texture of her thick, undercooked chapattis, which had caused me a permanent childhood stomach ache. Suppressing my revulsion, I swallowed the dal and the rice and the sliced radishes, then carefully gargled and washed the turmeric stains from under my fingernails before setting off for Wee Nooke.

I had not been to Wee Nooke for over fifteen years now. It is situated high on the hill, near Snow View, and is accessible only after a steep climb. When I reached the flats

I was already exhausted. I was in no shape to walk up, and thought wistfully of my Mercedes which had returned to Delhi. It wouldn't have been able to tackle the climb anyway.

I am uneasy with horses. There was no recourse but to engage a dandi. The idea of me, a civil servant, employed currently by the International Relief Organization, ascending the hills in a dusty khaki palanquin, held aloft by four or perhaps five tubercular men, appealed not at all. But the alternative was even more unattractive. Exhaustion, angina, a heart attack...perhaps I could phone the nephew and meet him in the flats. Or the club. But of course he didn't have a telephone, and I found myself negotiating, even bargaining, about the fare up. The dandi-walas had sized me up astutely and demanded seventy-five rupees. I held out at fifty, but to no avail. It would, they pointed out, work out to only ten rupees apiece, and we agreed to renegotiate when we arrived at our destination.

So here I was, returning home, like a king of yore, or even Idi Amin, except that these were no bwanas who were wheezing under my burden. Acutely conscious of the irony of my situation, I attempted to enter into an ingratiating conversation with them.

They were Dotyals, from Doti on the Nepal border, and I held forth about their historical and demographic migratory patterns into Kumaon.

The Dotyal nearest to me, on my right, the only one, I suspected, who could hear or was paying any heed to anything I said, muttered, 'That's all very well, but I'd like to stop for a beedi.'

They put me down unceremoniously, like a bundle, and settled themselves upon the rocks by the roadside to smile and smoke and gossip. The rough rhythmical sounds of their conversation mingled with the screeching film music from a radio in the garden of the house below.

At first I was patient, and gazed at the blue sky, and the incredible monsoon greenery, and the birds keetering above. A man wearing a Gandhi topi, a black coat and white cotton pyjamas, with an umbrella slung across his shoulders in the Pahari fashion, stopped to ask me the time.

A few whitewashed outhouses stood huddled near the road. One of them was roofless. The tin sheets on the other roofs were weighted down by stones. Below us, the township was fast encroaching upon what had once been woodland. There were rows upon tightly packed rows of flat-roofed cement buildings, with extruding vertical girders for future expansion. The gutter beside me was crowded with toffee papers and plastic bags, non-biodegradable emblems of progress.

A child walked past, clutching his mother's hand, and pointed at me curiously. I felt silly, incongruous and utterly helpless, strapped to my triangular papoose, marooned by the side of the road.

'I'll walk the rest of the way myself,' I said petulantly, struggling to step out of the dandi. In a second I was surrounded by five very angry men.

'Listen,' said the one I had been trying to converse with. 'Give us seventy-five rupees and go. It's a sin to steal from the poor. Even if we are illiterate, we earn by the honest sweat of our brow, working harder than any roadside donkey. Don't think you can fool us by your big talk.'

'But I settled for fifty,' I remonstrated, 'and I'm from Nainital—a local man.'

That drew a round of derisive laughter.

'I'm sure you must be, Maharaj,' another Dotyal said, in a tone that sounded amicable enough on the surface. But there was something about his eyes. 'And I'm sure you think that gives you the right to be carried up for free.' He spat contemptuously onto the roof of the house below.

I retreated, shamed and rejected, into my palanquin, and thus held aloft arrived at Wee Nooke.

WEE NOOKE

From the age of ten until I was twenty-two Wee Nooke had been my retreat, my haven, my sanctuary, my passage into the outside world. It had represented all that was desirable and attainable in life. It had contained books, a telephone and a radiogram. It was here that I had been moulded by Hiranand Headmaster's dreams and ambitions into the man I am today.

I passed the familiar moss-covered stone pillars that had once supported wrought iron gates. The gates now lay dismantled and rusting by a pile of dried cow dung pats.

Then I saw the beloved magnolia tree of my youth, under whose branches I had briefly known the textures of Parvati's hair, and the smell of her skin, which was the smell of magnolias. The tree was still there, as was most of the garden, only now a line of washing was strung across it: saris and blouses and brassieres and petticoats and underwear, all of which seemed brazen and sacrilegious in what had always been for me a bachelor's house, where Hiranand Headmaster's clothes, and Parvati's when she was there, had always dried modestly in the field behind the house.

I could remember, relive, helping her dry her saris, each of us holding one end of the length of cotton; the fine spray of soapy-smelling water that would splatter me as we flapped the sari dry; the sense of ritual as we laid it on the rocky grass. It felt like yesterday. I found myself staring foolishly at the circular stitches on a brassiere that dangled on the rope before me, as though at the contours on a topographical map, when Pooran Paper emerged to greet me.

Pooran is of medium height, and has a thin clever face, with deep laughter lines running from his fine nostrils to the edges of his narrow unsmiling lips. He was dressed in black trousers and a brown jacket, both shiny from wear. He wore socks and flip-flop slippers. His palms were clammy upon contact as he stepped forward to shake hands with me, the tips of his fingers stained brown with nicotine.

'Hullo, Mukul da,' he said, a little uncertainly, 'welcome to Wee Nooke.'

He hurried inside the house, leaving me alone in the garden, and then hurried out again, a chair in either hand. I recognized the chairs instantly. They were the two folding chairs that had stood by the wall in Hiranand Headmaster's study, next to the felt-covered desk littered with books and blotting paper. I did not recognize the objects that he brought out next, two occasional tables moulded in plastic to look like giant dice. His wife Neera emerged from behind him. He got her a chair as well, one of the tall dining-table chairs, backed with cane.

I examined her unabashedly. Hiranand Headmaster's envenomed epistles had made me curious about Neera, for they had overflowed with a bitterness so constant and ceaseless that I could not imagine what this slatternly figure could have done to occasion it.

Flesh bulged from underneath her tight black blouse, which seemed to thrust her breasts almost to her chin. She wore a violently patterned nylon sari, and had very small hands and feet, chapped and somehow raw-looking. Black button eyes gleamed in an apple-red face. Her dark curly waist-length hair was damp and uncombed. There was a towel draped around her shoulders, and she kept tossing her hair about to get the moisture out.

'What will you have?' she asked me. 'Hot or cold?'

I said I would welcome some tea. Coffee as served in the hills is not quite coffee.

'Lachhua! Where are you?' she shouted in the direction of the house. 'Lachhua! Are you dead, then?'

It was Irra who emerged from the shadowy veranda, looking very grave and composed, as her mother Parvati had used to look. But when she joined her palms in greeting I saw that she had still the hands of a child, tender and ink-stained.

I had already cast Neera as a villainess, but here she was, asking Irra in a disconcertingly gentle voice whether she would like some tea. Irra nodded curtly, and continued to stare unsmilingly at me, her foot tracing circular patterns in the stony moss-covered garden. I returned her stare, but she would simply not look at, only through me. I gave up the exercise.

Neera disappeared towards the house, and Irra followed her. Pooran and I fell into conversation. He had an endearing, respectful manner, and talked well. He seemed in every way a personable young man. I wondered why Hiranand

Headmaster had been prejudiced against him to the extent of disinheriting him, leaving him homeless if not penniless.

'He had become a little senile towards the end, senile and very bitter,' Pooran Paper said, as though reading my thoughts. 'Your letters were the only thing he lived for, your letters and his dinner. He had become obsessed by food, he was always complaining about Neera's cooking. Then he would overeat, and insist that she was poisoning him, so that we could inherit his wealth.' He smiled wryly, and the laughter lines across his cheeks became even more pronounced. He lit a cigarette and puffed at it as though it were a hookah.

'Your letters, and his dinner. "Each day has become like a mountain," he would complain. He would wait for the postman all morning. No one else ever wrote to him. "Only Mukul Nainwal didn't let me down," he would always say. "Only Mukul Nainwal." You were successful by his standards. You had not betrayed your promise,' Pooran said to me, almost accusingly. He paused for a moment to wipe his nose upon his sleeve.

'As for me, he hated me because I work for a Hindi newspaper. Call it a paper or a newsletter, it is meant to inform and educate Paharis about their heritage. Too many people from the plains in Kumaon these days. Do you know that we have a negative birth rate? Just like Sweden and other advanced countries! These plains people think of us Paharis as a race of servants. He hated my paper.

'"Hindi is a language of slaves," he would say, although Sanskrit was all right for him.

'"It's English which is the language of slaves," I would reply, but I didn't like to irritate him because then he would trouble Neera. He was almost completely senile, you see.' Pooran seemed almost to be apologizing for the dead man.

'Tell me about your paper,' I said, for I was already beginning to feel a little guilty about all the lives I would have to dislocate in deference to Hiranand Headmaster's last wishes. Pooran Paper was a fascinating conversationalist. He told me about his paper, the *Himalayan Times*, and talked knowledgeably of the fuelwood crisis, deforestation, soil erosion and changing weather patterns. He waxed eloquent on terrace farming, micro hydroelectric power and the Chipko movement.

'Do you realize that the entire Himalayan ecosystem is under siege?' he asked fiercely. Lighting yet another cigarette, he told me about the Pindari glacier which was retreating at the rate of thirteen metres annually. 'Annually!' he thundered. 'Do you know what that means? Annually means every year! The Pindari glacier is retreating by thirteen metres every year!'

I was charmed. This was the Third World I approved of, the Third World of UNIDO brochures, first-hand. He even wanted to interview me for his paper. 'We like to know that our hill people are moving on in the world,' he said deferentially.

We were on our third cup of tea by now. The sky was overcast, and there were thunderous black clouds over China Peak. I glanced at my gold-plated Seiko watch, which Adeleine had presented to me on my last birthday. It was only four in the afternoon.

He saw me glancing at my watch. 'Would you like to see the library?' he asked, and led me into a little lean-to where the veranda had been covered up and converted into a small annexe. The green painted wood had already begun to rot at the sides. The door opened with some difficulty and revealed a dark, cobwebbed room with broken windowpanes and a single dim bulb. The room housed four glass-fronted cupboards, the doors of which did not quite shut.

As I leaned forward to look at the books, I stumbled over an inert body lying upon the floor. A startled cry escaped me, which turned into a scream as I discovered that my ankle was caught in a tight claw-like grip.

Pooran prodded the body with his foot. 'Lachhua,' he said, in the sort of voice I have heard village women use with their livestock, '*hut, Lachhua, hut.*'

The thing let go of my leg, and stood up. My heart missed yet another beat as I examined the apparition before me. It was a young boy of about fifteen, with a vacant, evil face, one side of which was convoluted into a permanent paralytic grin. His arms, one of which was longer than the other, arched out at a little distance from his body, and the hands were splayed and disoriented. He was dressed in torn blue pyjamas and a white shirt, and his hair was covered with cobwebs.

'*Hut, Lachhua,*' Pooran said again, not unkindly, and prodded him out of the room. I watched amazed.

'Lachhua helps Neera around the house,' Pooran Paper said in explanation, 'and he used to look after Hiranand Headmaster as well. He is a little retarded, but very energetic.'

I examined the books with exaggerated interest so as not to betray my horror. They seemed promising. Many of them were quite old, and possibly valuable. A musty smell overflowed into the room as I handled them.

'That window,' I said reproachfully to Pooran, 'it should

have been repaired. Moisture can damage these books.'
Already, my words held a proprietary ring. I scrutinized the
shelves greedily. There were a great many textbooks, and
the collected works of George Bernard Shaw, Bertrand
Russel and Ibsen, besides several out of date encyclopaedias.
Although there was not sufficient light to inspect them
properly, I could already spot a few treasures. There were
three volumes of Atkinson's *Himalayan Gazetteer* in what
appeared a fairly early imprint, and a dog-eared edition of
Man Eaters of Kumaon, inscribed and signed by Jim Corbett
in a small, precise hand.

There were several other curiosities. I unearthed a
handsomely bound copy of *A Servant of John Company*,
published in 1897 from Calcutta and London. A monocled
portrait of the author adorned the frontispiece. The paper
felt smooth and young, and the ink was still vibrant with
exposition.

I wheezed with joy, and stored my discoveries upon the
window ledge before reconnoitering farther. As I was
scooping out yet another volume of Atkinson, my shoe
squelched upon a frog that had wandered in. It let out a
terrible cry as it leapt frenziedly about the room. I hurriedly
gathered up the handful of books I had collected, and rushed
out of the room, inhaling the fresh air outside in quick,
nervous gulps.

DRAMATIS PERSONAE

Neera brought me yet another cup of tea, and some quite delectable samosas and jalebis. Pooran dusted the books, which were crawling with silverfish, and wrapped them in newspapers and packed them into a plastic bag for me.

Their sons, Sonu and Sunil, returned from Mallital full of the details of some exciting football match. They made a pleasant tableau of family life, and it disturbed me that I should be the unwitting agent of its disruption. I said as much.

'Oh no, Mukul daju,' Pooran protested. 'I understand your, position. And a house—what is it but a shelter from the elements? It's only a roof, and we will soon find another. I'm a socialist in my principles. We will be able to afford only a small flat now, just a room probably, or perhaps a two-room set. There are some under construction near Ramsay Hospital. There won't be any space for Irra now, but you will do something for her, I'm sure. After all, many a swallow can feed on a rich man's leftovers.'

The entire problem of Irra's existence was thus deftly hurled in my direction, so deftly and swiftly that there was nothing I could do to dodge it. She had been standing right behind me, listening unblinkingly to the exchange. I noticed she had pubescent breasts, and hated myself for the thought, for I suspected there was something illicit in it. Her hair was braided into two tight plaits which reached down to her shoulders. She did not respond at all to the conversation, but continued to stare at me, until I got faintly irritated by her scrutiny.

'Of course, she has her uncle,' Pooran continued in a sarcastic tone. And then, seeing my surprised look, 'Pushpendra Pande—he's a lawyer. And a liar, if I may be permitted to say so.'

'Pushpendra is Parvati's cousin from her father's side. He is only twenty-eight, but old as the hills when it comes to cunning,' Pooran Paper said. There was a watchful look in his eyes. I had the uneasy feeling that I was being somehow manipulated or played upon. 'And then he has married a Rajput, a Bisht girl who ran away from her first husband to marry him!'

'Good for him!' I found myself saying. Pooran stared at me, surprised and I glared back. Violent emotions gripped at my throat. 'Someone in your family needed to teach you lot a lesson! Caste, caste, caste—but then, I suppose there isn't much else left for you to be proud of! My wife isn't a Brahmin. Oh no, not even a Nandhoti Brahmin! No, she is Burmese, half Burmese and half English. The same English who once ruled you! And what happened to your pride before them? Don't tell me, I know!'

I was horrified by my outburst but I didn't seem to be

able to stop myself. Now I turned upon Irra. 'Your grand-uncle Hiranandji, who has left me this house now—he was the same man who prevented me from marrying your mother! He wouldn't allow me to marry her. He mated her to that tubercular Lalit instead because his genes were right. And should I tell you more? I'm grateful to him, glad I didn't marry her, thankful I escaped from these wretched hills.'

I was appalled and mortified by my behaviour, but I couldn't help myself. The hurt had been malingering within me far too long, for a quarter century now.

*

It had happened a long time ago. I had told my mother of my hopes, and then brought up the subject with Hiranand Headmaster that very afternoon, amidst the mess of uncorrected examination papers and unsigned school reports in his study.

'So you, Sir Mukul Nainwal, wish to pledge your troth to my niece, Kumari Parvati Pant,' he had said. His expression was uncommunicative, the face he wore while scoring a schoolboy's essays.

'You leave for Allahabad tomorrow, do you not? I shall communicate with you by post, and let you know of my decision.'

I left for Allahabad. When the letter arrived it had '72½' written upon the flap, indicating that any unauthorized person who opened and read it would have committed a sin equivalent to the murder of as many brahmins as would have worn 72½ maunds of sacred threads. It contained within it the word 'miscegenation'. 'Do not misunderstand me,' the neat, precise handwriting had said, 'it is not that I myself subscribe to these antiquated theories, or believe in caste or creed, but it is always wise to remain within the circumscribed circle of social acceptance, especially for a woman.'

Putting the letter away I had laid down and wept for a long time. Then I fell asleep. When I awoke I read it again. 'Although she is my niece, I am also not entirely convinced (apart from that other consideration) that she is a suitable partner for you. You know full well what hopes I cherish for you and I am certain you shall respect and abide by my decision.' It had ended, 'Affly, Hiranand Joshi'.

For centuries we Khasiya Brahmins had lived in these hills, ploughing the earth in honest labour, and pursuing our Brahminical duties. We wore short dhotis and were proud to work in the fields, for we loved the soil and the land of our forefathers.

Then these Thuldhoties had arrived from the plains, and declared that they, and only they, among the twice-born Brahmins, were entitled to power and position. These Pants from Maharashtra, these Pandes and Joshis from Kannauj were all courtiers and sycophants by class and occupation. They affected long dhotis to signify their superior intellectual and social status, and scorned the labour of the fields or the tending of the shrines.

I did not feel inferior just because I could not reel off my 'Sakha' or my 'Pravara'. Although my grandfather was just a Phulariya Brahmin, I knew that my grandmother had been a Thuldhoti, a Pant from Uparora. I had never told Hiranand Headmaster that, I had been too proud, too proud and too certain it could not matter to him.

Hiranand Headmaster read George Bernard Shaw and

Bertrand Russell and Rabindranath Tagore. Yet when he learnt of my love, after I had confided my dreams to him, he wrote me that letter, and within a week settled Parvati's marriage to Lalit, who had been my best friend. Lalit was a Thuldhoti, after all.

When I saw Parvati next, she was already engaged to Lalit. 'But of course I could never have married you,' she said, quite casually, in the middle of a conversation. I never forgave her the tone in which she said it, and why it had been axiomatic that she could not. I forgave Hiranand Headmaster his letter, but I carried her rejection all my life.

My mother never questioned me about it. It was a wound which I nursed with devotion, a hurt which was to mingle in time with another rejection, my alienation from home and India. It never ceased to trouble me that I made good not here but elsewhere, until my love for Parvati and for my homeland combined into a single dull pain, the constant grieving pain of jealous and jilted lovers.

*

My mouth was dry, I was gasping. I had no idea that those wounds still festered. I thought of Adeleine and counted until ten. 'I'm sorry,' I said, 'I'm sorry, I did not mean all that. I was upset, I overreacted. May I have a glass of water, please?'

But Pooran was not upset, nor Irra, who was still staring at me in that blank inscrutable way. Neera was placidly gathering the clothes from the line into little heaps and carrying them in.

I went in to wash my face, and realized for the first time how incredibly dilapidated the house had become. Only two of the main rooms were still inhabited, or even habitable. The gloomy room near the kitchen must have been Hiranand Headmaster's, and the other appeared to be occupied by Pooran and his family. Clothes and school books were flung everywhere, and there seemed to be no fixed place for eating, for there were plates and tumblers on every window sill and table. In the bathroom, the windowpanes were smashed and broken and boarded up with cardboard. The flush did not work.

Hiranand Headmaster had been very house-proud. I could not imagine him in these surroundings. I realized that we had been sitting outside not only to enjoy the sunshine but also because Pooran was too embarrassed to seat me inside.

Neera had brought me water and yet more tea. Irra was still sitting outside. Now, as I gulped my fourth cup of tea and readied myself to leave, she darted wordlessly in and returned with a satchel and a small suitcase. 'Shall we go, then?' she asked unsmilingly, as though the matter was quite settled.

I was so shamed by my recent loss of self-control that I did not know how to respond. I turned to Pooran for aid, but the afternoon was rapidly turning to dusk and I could not read his expression.

His wife came to my rescue. 'What's the hurry, Irra, we can sort things out slowly,' she said. 'Why don't you walk down to town with Mukul da? Take a torch with you, and get my blouse from the tailor on the way back.' She went in and got us a torch, and an umbrella in case it rained, and behaved, all said and done, like a sensible and dignified woman.

They seemed to have both taken their dispossession very lightly. It must be the clear mountain air, I decided, which kept them so unworldly.

AN EVENING WALK

My adoptive daughter-to-be and I set out on the climb down. Irra suggested that we take a short cut. The sight of the broken craggy path before us filled me with dismay, but I did not want to expose my timidity.

It was a beautiful evening. The intense evanescent crimson of the sky filtered through the greying dusk around us. The cows were returning home, their bells tinkling gently. They were sure-footed, calm and certain of their destinations as they made their elliptical way across the steep hillside. The deep, sad wail of a conch shell broke the air, followed closely by the brief trembling of a prayer bell, as a window lit up in the old, damp house to our right. A figure stood silhouetted at the window, brooding at us.

'That is my friend Beena's mother,' Irra told me. 'Beena ran away to Haldwani to catch a train to Bombay to become a film star, but they caught her. Neera di does not let me play with her any more.'

I asked her what she would do when she grew up. Would she leave the hills as well?

'I wish to be a doctor,' she replied firmly, her eyebrows knit tight in concentration, the faint down on her upper lip straining at a suppressed smile. 'I don't care where I live as long as I join the medical line. Perhaps I could go to America. I have been to Lucknow twice.' We walked on.

'But Pooran daju says that the people in the plains cannot be trusted,' she volunteered next.

'And what do you feel?' I asked, glad to find her so talkative.

'Well,' she said seriously, switching on her torch to reveal a freshly laid pat of cow dung. 'Pooran daju cannot be trusted. You had better be careful with him. I am alone in the world, you know, so I have learnt to be careful. Perhaps people in the plains are even worse.' She snivelled philosophically. I could not draw any more out of her, but I felt there was something ungrateful and unchildlike about her observation.

A young ghasyaran slid down the hillside just ahead of us, and another giggling figure slithered down after her. They stood before us briefly, two happy young girls in their bright blue petticoats and heavy silver jewellery. Then they adjusted the bundles of freshly scythed grass on their heads and walked on, confident and sure-footed as the cows. Mentally, I compared their barefooted, carefree, though doubtless poverty-stricken existence with the quite different sorrows of the child before me. Her forehead was furrowed in thought, her small figure tense and determined, as she led the way with the Eveready torch.

We had almost reached our destination now, and only a small jump separated us from the main road. The rains had made the soil weak. The path gave way beneath me, the mountains turned to mud, and I hurtled down to find myself heaped upon a bed of nettles that grew by the side of the road.

I had grazed my arms, and my legs were stinging through the thin summer suit. Feeling clumsy and foolish, I tried to sit up as though there was nothing much the matter.

My fall transformed Irra. She was solicitous and maternal. 'I will get you some palak leaves, they work as an antidote,' she said, helping me tenderly to my feet. Then a note of doubt crept into her voice. 'It's a sin to pluck leaves after sunset, it's their bedtime,' she whispered, and stared anxiously at me, awaiting my guidance.

I had no response to offer, but she seemed to have reached a decision. She beamed her torch about until she found some palak leaves, which she knelt down to pluck. She applied them gently to my stinging arms.

When I felt her firm, loving child's touch I knew she had made her private choice, and I had to make mine. I realized that she was the daughter of the only woman I had ever truly loved, and that I had no option but to be responsible for her.

Irra did not want to come all the way to the hotel, and we parted outside the tailor's shop in Malli Bazaar. The bazaar is crowded, winding and cheerful, deflecting here and there into even narrower cobbled by-lanes. I remembered and recognized many of the shops. The Allied Stores, Sardar Wool House, Rais Brothers, The London Cloth House. Even the exteriors were unchanged.

A sense of déjà vu overtook me, as, walking along, I glimpsed what appeared to be a new generation of the very same faces I had known so many years ago. It was like a time inversion, for they all looked like younger replicas of their parents as I had known them. 'Does nothing change here, then,' I thought irritably, 'except to become tawdrier and more decayed?'

I arrived at Green Cafe, haunt of our youth, where, over tea and kachauris, we had discussed college elections, and Nehru's policies, and why Dev Anand did not marry Suraiyya. There was nothing Green about it, only a garish red-and-white signboard and a promise of dim lighting and filth within. I went in like a sleepwalker, but I was not the same person now as I had been then. I could no more sit here alone and eat over-fried kachauris than I could stroll into the harbour slums in Hong Kong and mix with the boat people there.

My term in Hong Kong was due to be over in a year. I had applied for a transfer to an underdeveloped African country, to complete my range of experience for a book I was contemplating. I was, in a modest way, an expert on poverty. I was versed in the gradations of lack, want and need, aware that excess is itself a form of deprivation.

Yet, the poverty of other people is very different from the privations of one's youth, and it had not of course seemed like poverty then, but rather the apotheosis of high living. I was ashamed of my snobbery, and resolutely re-entered Green Cafe, and ordered tea and a plate of potato tikkis and allowed myself to think of many things I had been trying all my life to forget.

PITAJI, MASTERJI

I thought of my father. I have a memory of being carried astride his shoulders down a quiet road and my mother following behind. I had found myself suddenly eye level with waving shady green leaves and known and savoured what was surely happiness. He had left us when I was four, without even a photograph. He renounced my mother, me and the world to become a sadhu. We never saw him again. We always talked about him as though he were already dead. A relative told me when I was twelve that someone had met him at a temple near Badrinath. I did not tell my mother.

My mother was tall, broad, slow and stupid. She smelt of cows' milk, cow dung and hard work. She never discussed the hopes she must have reposed in me.

We had a cow and received rent from a shop which my father had owned. It had been let out to a barber, who later bought it from my mother before she died, all alone. I wondered if he were still alive. I asked the hovering waiter what had happened to Yakub, the barber with hennaed hair and a shop in Tallital. He was confused by the question, and, impressed with my Hong Kong aura, rushed to ask the proprietor. Yakub had died last year, I was informed, and his son had opened a dry-cleaner's shop instead.

I thought of the other dead man, who tried to make me his son, then married his niece Parvati to Lalit because he feared miscegenation. I should never have seen him again. I should have killed him and strangled the constipated matchstick of a body, smashed his cerebrum, destroyed the tyranny of gratitude by which he bound us all. But we were all beaten and bribed and exhausted, even Lalit to whom he had gifted Parvati. Now it was her daughter Irra who was burdened with the same charity. At least she seemed aware of its price.

But this anger was too disturbing. I assumed instead a comfortably cynical mental posture, and thought amusedly of placid Pooran and his socialist principles. The reason why Pooran had no bitterness, I told myself complacently, was because Hiranand Headmaster had never reached out for his soul. It was me he had sought, Mukul Nainwal, fatherless, questing, burdened with the shame of parental inadequacy.

I had received private tuition from him in the evenings. After school we would walk together to Wee Nooke. I would carry his books, hurrying to keep pace with his thin mean stride. The school was only a short distance from his house. My mind has all but expelled it from memory for it has caused me more misery than I can bear to remember. We would walk home together, Hiranand Headmaster and I, past the sports pavilion and the deserted playing fields. The boys would laugh and push and rush past us. The masters would smile down at me as they stopped to talk to him.

People rarely locked their houses in the hills then, but he

would fiddle suspiciously with three keys before the dark teak door groaned open. I would stare at the gloomy furniture outlined within as though at the geography of death. He would take off his topi and perch it on the hatstand near the door. We would creep together through the dim hallway to his study, where he would first switch on the light and then remove his circular gold-rimmed spectacles and place them opposite the inkstand on his desk, exactly parallel to the pink blotting pad and diagonal to the ivory timepiece.

This done, he would consider the room with keen interest, as though convinced it would have something new to offer his scrutiny. After he had examined every cobweb, he would march in a stooped funereal step towards the kitchen, and return carrying two cups of tea and a plate of circularly arranged Marie biscuits on a tray printed with a bright but fading pattern of lovebirds.

Later, when Parvati kept house, she would serve us samosas and jalebis and dalmoth, but he would invariably send her back for biscuits. He would even nibble at them circularly, and having consumed three Marie biscuits, half arise from his seat to brush the crumbs from his suit.

Teatime over, we would go through the day's lessons. It was the year 1946, and the British empire still crowded the pages of Bartholomew's Atlas. Hiranand Headmaster fancied himself a Gentleman and an Imperialist, and thought poorly of Mohandas Karamchand Gandhi. 'Gandhi! A Gujarati and a bania!' he would snort. 'A Gujarati bania without a banian! Now tell me, where is Tanganyika?' Again we would encounter the omnipresent red of the British empire— Zanzibar, Mount Kilimanjaro, Lake Victoria.

'Very good, my boy!...Nehru's all right though, an aristocrat. After all, blood will tell.' I should have known even then that ten years later he would spell out the word miscegenation and refuse me his niece Parvati's hand in marriage.

We would start on English grammar. Pursing his lips, sniffing at his fingernails, he would put on the self-satisfied smirk he wore during morning assembly.

'A single shelf of a good European library is worth the whole native literature of India and Arabia! Now who said that, my boy? Macauley, it was Macauley! Thomas Babington Macauley! The man who brought Education to our country!'

'And what else did Macauley say?' he would ask me fiercely. 'What did he say that I constantly repeat to you, Mukul Nainwal?'

I had no reply.

'Macauley said, "We must do our best to form a class who may be interpreters between us and the millions whom we govern—a class of persons, Indian in blood and colour, but English in taste and opinions, in morals and in intellect!"'

His voice would be shrill and his eyes bright with happy excitement, and I would watch the spit dribble down the side of his mouth.

We would switch to poetry, his voice gaining in velocity and resonance, while I suppressed an urgent desire to pee.

'IF—you can meet with Triumph and Disaster, and treat the two impostors just the same,

'IF you can bear to hear the truth you have spoken twisted to make a trap for fools...'

He would strut through the entire remainder of the

poem, pacing the worn red-and-black Afghan carpet, mispronouncing the words, mangling the metre. As he rushed towards the conclusion in a Churchillian roar, his voice would echo across the dark, quiet hills, while the silence whistled in the pine trees outside.

'If you can fill the unforgiving minute
with sixty seconds worth of distance run
Yours is the Earth and everything that's in it.
And—which is more—you will be a man, my son!'

His fingers would rumple my hair as he approached the 'my son' bit. I could see and hear the exclamation mark suspended somewhere between the felt-covered desk and the grainy light bulb while the shadows warred upon the walls.

The urgency afflicting my urogenital muscles would already be deadening into a still pain.

'What is "If", my boy?'

My face by now would be purple with tension.

'Noun, verb or clause?'

Some inner clock would warn him of the hour even before the ivory timepiece did, and he would leave the room a split second before the six evening chimes tinkled falsely into that grim interior.

'Clause!' he would bark over his shoulder as he left for the kitchen to attend to the dinner.

Abandoning the maths exercises he had set me, I would rush out into the pebbled garden and gleefully pee upon the drooping hydrangeas.

He would not employ a cook. A middle-aged Muslim woman lived in the erstwhile biwikhana attached to the house, and she would do all the chores and often cook his meals as well. The boys in school sniggered that she was his mistress, and my mother would entreat with me never to eat anything she had cooked. Hiranand Headmaster was himself of course above all such needs and prejudices.

He fancied himself as a cook. He had a somewhat limited repertoire, for he could do a mutton curry and caramel custard, and not much else. The meat (he called it shikar) would be ritually prepared on a hot plate in the dining room. Redolent with onions and garlic, it would stew for hours in an enormous brass pot, rocking and rumbling and steamily clouding the glass surface on the group photograph of the headmasters' conference, where Hiranand Joshi stood posing stiffly, second to the left, before a Corinthian balustrade.

At the table, the conversation would chart his favourite subjects—his love for the hills and his contempt for hillmen. He had never been to England, but every anecdote would end with a hallelujah to the white man.

'Now look at the Britishers,' he would say, sucking noisily at the marrow of a long yellow bone, 'now that's a fine race of men.'

All Paharis and hillmen were 'jackals'. A special hatred was reserved for nationalists and politicians. 'All your khadi topi Independence-walas and their followers are nothing but thieves and pickpockets, and that's why they love those processions, and waving those placards. The police are unnecessarily making heroes out of them,' he would declare, clanging the clean long bone on the cracked dinner plate for emphasis.

The hatred was rivalled only by the animus he harboured against the fashionable missionary boarding schools, whose principals had once resisted his inclusion in the executive committee at a local headmasters' conference. 'Servants of the padres' was how he referred to them, but I think he was a little envious of the closed shop of the Irish fathers and other white missionaries, and felt inadequate before their long strides and flowing cassocks. Our school had better equipped science labs, and our teachers were paid better, but we were Anglo-Vernacular, and government funded, so the true public school tradition was always denied to us.

Hiranand Headmaster believed passionately in Western Empirical Thought. 'Science and Fact are all that should remain sacred in Modern India,' he would declaim, while I wondered what to tell my mother when I got home. Often I would be forced to eat two dinners.

He wrote to Jawaharlal Nehru expressing his views on Science as the true religion of modern India. Nehru had replied back, saying that, as an educationist, and as someone living in the Himalayas, 'you will doubtless agree that the Spirit of Mankind, which discovered Science, and utilized Fact, is inaccessible to both, except through itself.' Hiranand Headmaster told me that he had written to George Bernard Shaw as well, discussing Evolutionary Socialism, but received no reply. Perhaps he had been mean with the postage.

Hiranand Headmaster used me mercilessly as his spy and stooge with the boys and masters, although with my Pahari naiveté I was for the most part innocent of these purposes. I would be the first to tell him about Mahesh Belwal tearing King George the Fifth's portrait from the encyclopaedia in an excess of nationalistic feeling, or about the side business Harish Adhikari had established with supposedly broken test tubes. I would receive a sermon on Honesty as reward. Of course it did not take the other students long to catch on my perfidy.

Everyone hated me. I was known as 'the Collaborator' and the title followed me even to college in Allahabad. The boys used me for misinformation or simply to pull Hiranand Headmaster's hateful leg. Once Mahesh Belwal imprisoned me in the toilet for an entire afternoon, and made me drink cow's urine and swear loyalty to a calendar portrait of the abhorred Gandhi. I can still recall the sweet, viscous taste of warmish fluid, the toothless smile on the calendar photograph, the salt of my tears, the hysterical laughter of triumphant schoolboys.

I never told Hiranand Headmaster of the pain his attentions caused me. I remained pathetically grateful for the occasional communicative look, the private pat, the sharing of information and opinion, the belief in a future, the mere sanctuary of a home.

College and Allahabad opened up an entirely new world. Away from the shadow of being Hiranand Headmaster's collaborator, I discovered for a while the dizzying joys of camaraderie. I made friends and laughed and clowned and got clumsily drunk. Although it was Hiranand Headmaster who had insisted that I study in Allahabad and not stay on at Nainital, a part of me began actively hating him. Nevertheless, in my weekly letters to him (intended, obliquely, also for Parvati), I would don another mask altogether. I was always to be the one apart, earnest and ambitious, scorning those that I admired, admiring those that I scorned.

It was around then that I started idolizing the poet Hasrat Rampuri. Hasrat was the head of the department of English at Allahabad University, and the foremost Urdu poet of the day. The more pointedly he snubbed and ignored my hero worship, the more grateful I would become at being spared his patronage. I began to learn the joys of disaffection. I would pretend even to mock him, and to underplay my feelings generally. Even my love for Parvati, romantic and sentimental though it was, became conserved into a more tender and quiet emotion, at least on the surface.

Parvati married Lalit, and I lived out Hiranand Headmaster's ambitions, and became a moderately successful man. A woman friend in Hong Kong (we had a brief sexual entanglement) once told me mockingly that I was suffering an unresolved Childhood Romance. I had resisted the phrase. I am a happy man, I told myself, a very happy man, a very successful man.

I longed suddenly for Adeleine's unemotional presence. I was exhausted by so much reminiscence. She would never have allowed me to even touch the soggy-looking potato tikkis which Green Cafe had provided without first checking out the kitchen. Neither she nor her mother had ever set foot in the Indian quarter in Rangoon.

Yet Adeleine was emotional in her way, she wept for Sue-Ellen in Dallas, and leafed through her dead husband's letters in a way I knew signified love. Perhaps that was the reason why Hiranand Headmaster had chosen to love me, I thought: I was just as unlovable and unloved as he was.

I paid the bill, and told myself that I was blaming a dead man, who had left me all he had, for my own middle-aged inadequacies.

I remembered some beloved lines of Hasrat's verses. The poetry of the Persian tongues did not come easily to my Hong Kong habituated officialese, but soon the words flowed, sinuous as serpents, plumed as birds of paradise, haunting as houris. They had to do with a texture of evening unknown to the English language; they evoked the spirit of memory and the timeless Indian dusk, when the low smoke swirls from cow dung and charcoal fires.

Chimneyless Pahari houses had been another pet subject of Hiranand Headmaster's ire. 'Do you want to understand the stupidity of our hill people?' he would exclaim. 'They could not conceive or invent the chimney without the help of the Angrez! Yes, my boy, it was the English who brought the chimney to our houses!'

HIGH SOCIETY

As I was thus stumbling and dreaming, I met the three brothers ambling through the bazaar. Mohan Mischief, Sohan Selfish and Jeewan Jaundice were all dressed in identical blue blazers with shiny brass buttons. They persuaded me to join them at the club, insisting that I come, not taking no for an answer. I had the pleasant feeling that I was to be shown off.

I must confess that the Boat House club had awed me in my youth. Although, after our tryst with destiny, membership had been thrown open for Indians, I knew no club-walas. It was of course different now. I had seen the world. I had out-wogged my wildest ambitions. I was an International Civil Servant in the Crown Colony of Hong Kong.

We made our way through dilapidated cane furniture, past fading unfixed photographs and sagging sofas to the desolate bar. The unpolished wooden floors were covered with tattered jute matting. Everything in sight bespoke better days. Amidst this pathetic residue of colonial glory, we made a forlorn foursome around the inert fireplace.

A rather magnificent old woman was sitting alone at the window seat near the bar. A glass of whisky trembled in her beringed hands. Fair as any European, she was dressed in a pink-and-silver brocade sari.

'Who is that delicious looking young man with you?' she asked Sohan, in a very loud, very Mayfair voice.

'That is Mr Nainwal from Hong Kong,' Sohan replied triumphantly.

'Who?' she asked again. 'Do speak louder, please?'

'Mr Nainwal from Hong Kong,' Sohan Selfish screamed, exerting all the lung power at his command.

'Do give him my regards,' she said graciously. 'Really, one sees some quite nice people here sometimes.'

A tall thin man and a short fat man strolled in together, hand in hand. They were both brandishing swagger sticks. The fat person was wearing a checked cap, and the thin man had a leg set in a plaster cast. I was introduced to them with due propriety. The fractured leg belonged to the deputy inspector general of police, and the gentleman in the beret was the district magistrate, Nainital. They joined us, we talked and drank and munched peanuts. I felt once again like the local boy made good.

The peanuts were highly salted, and I asked for a glass of water.

The district magistrate wagged a remonstrative finger.

'I wouldn't allow any of that,' he said, 'You better keep off the aqua pura. Lake water, you know. Sewage. Most of us here suffer perennially from diarrhoea and worms.'

I flinched and had another gulp of whisky.

'I have even seen tapeworms in the intestines of dead fish,' he continued manfully.

I began feeling distinctly queasy, and was eyeing my glass with suspicion when a huge man glowing with good health strode into the room, followed by an exquisite Nepali-type beauty. His face appeared exceedingly familiar, but he recognized me before I did him. It was Harish Adhikari, who used to steal the test tubes. He had been known in his set as Harish How-Do-You-Do, and he subjected me to a vigorous handshake, and a bear hug as well, before settling himself comfortably on an ageing sofa nearby. Harish How-Do-You-Do was a forest contractor now. He ordered a round of drinks for us. His wife had a brandy with cola. They told me about their two sons, the holiday they had all spent together in Singapore, and their new eight-channel video cassette recorder.

Harish turned to the others, and, smiling his infectious childhood smile, said confidingly, 'Do you know what we called Nainwal in school? He was known as the Collaborator! He was the headmaster's blue-eyed boy! I was always getting into trouble because of him!'

I felt myself flushing. I was offended and mortified, although it was obviously not a serious remark. But he had not forgotten.

Harish How-Do-You-Do's wife kept signalling her boredom to him, but he paid no heed. 'You were a real hard-working bugger,' he said jocularly. 'I bet you never imagined that a fool like me might get on in life, kya?'

The conversation turned to a local politician, a Dom, an outcaste who had the backing of the ruling party.

'A Brahmin priest comes to conduct prayers in his house every day!' Mohan Mischief told the assembled company. 'I tell you, it's a scandal!'

'Really?' Harish How-Do-You-Do's wife said. She had a lovely ringing voice.

'Yes, even Brahmins do anything for money nowadays,' Sohan Selfish said sadly, 'anything for money!'

'Caste politics,' the district magistrate said sagely, 'nothing but caste politics.'

Someone ordered yet more whisky. I was drunk. The conversation veered to Hiranand Headmaster and his legacy. All Nainital, it appeared, was speculating about the use I would put Wee Nooke to. The obese district magistrate asked me if I was planning to establish an orphanage. The deputy inspector general of police said, no, it was going to be a mushroom farm, with imported Japanese technology.

And then I had a moment of intense clarity, the near apocalyptic understanding that overtakes a person before the final collapse into drunkenness. Hatred for my benefactor seared through my blood like a viscous presence. There was a sort of physical conflagration within my system. 'The impulse to Sanskritization always runs parallel to the impulse to Anglicization,' I said ponderously, articulating each word with great care. I felt I had finally arrived at an important truth. There was a buzzing sound in my ears. Then I doubled over with pain, and almost fainted.

Tears welled in my eyes. I coughed. Someone thumped my back. Concern was showered upon me like confetti. I wondered briefly if it was a heart attack. I tried to pray, but thought failed me. I could find no tongue in which to speak, until the wailing rhythms of a Cantonese television commercial came forth to soothe and comfort me. I sat up, smiled, and drank a glass of water, until even the residual emotion had subsided, and I was myself again.

'I used to visit the old bugger sometimes,' Harish said, 'not that he ever gave me the time of day, even after all these years. But we have a duty to our elders. There was no one at his funeral, they couldn't find four men to bring the body down. No, seriously, there was only his nephew Pooran, and that Pushpendra, Parvati's cousin. Pooran just didn't inform anybody.'

'Mukul had better be careful of that Pushpendra,' he continued, 'he is up to something, that's pukka. A seasoned goonda, that's what he is, and I can smell some crookery cooking. He and that Pooran Paper are plotting something together.'

'Pooran is a fine man,' I mumbled, for the whisky and the emotions had taken their toll, 'a very decent man.'

'Decent!' Harish How-Do-You-Do exclaimed contemptuously. 'Decent! After what he did to Parvati! Decent!' He turned to his wife. 'You tell Mukul what he did, it's not me that he will believe.'

'Why should we get involved in all this?' she said equably. 'Let's go home, Ji.'

'Lalit was Mukul's friend; now Hiranandji has left all his responsibilities upon him. I think he has a duty to know. Why, everyone in Nainital knows about what they did to Parvati! Why not Mukul?' he demanded.

Mohan daju was getting agitated too. 'Tell him, bhabhi,' he said to Harish's wife. 'He will believe you more than us.'

'You seem to know a lot about Parvati,' I said coldly, praying inwardly that they not dispossess me of my memories of her as she had been.

'If you don't mind my saying so in this exalted company,' Harish How-Do-You-Do continued, addressing the D.M.

and the D.I.G. with exaggerated respect, 'if I may be blunt, our friend Pooran Paper is a journalist. He lectures villagers, villagers who don't have a lota to use while shitting, about the problems of soil erosion! Conservation! Ecology! I agree it's necessary, but nowadays they make it seem as though it's better to let a man starve than to cut down a tree! But when these journalists need a loan, it's us, the wicked forest contractors, that they turn to. And then, Pooran Paper has the ear of the forestry minister. Shri Vishwajit Singh, minister for forests, jails, sports and animal husbandry! And we all know how much he loves trees, don't we?' he said, winking broadly at all seven of us, quite carried away by the flow of his own impassioned rhetoric.

'And why does Shri Vishwajit Singh love trees, pray? Because—' his eyes grew bloodshot and his voice rose to a roar—'BECAUSE, gentlemen, trees are felled into timber, and timber is made into pulp, and this pulp is converted in Nasik into crisp new rupee notes. And our friend Pooran loves trees, but he also loves the timber and the pulp and he loves those currency notes as well. And I love Pooran, and...'

His voice was echoing through the deserted club, the bearers were clattering the crockery, the D.M. was looking dismayed. Harish How-Do-You-Do's beautiful wife bustled him out, bidding us goodbye.

So, on the long climb back to the hotel, and through the hastily warmed dinner, I allowed myself to think once again of Parvati, as Jeewan and his brothers endeavoured to tell me what the world had done to her.

FIRST LOVE

The first time I met Parvati was when she had opened the door for me at Wee Nooke. Her pale face gleamed in the dark hallway like a waxy magnolia bloom.

There was something severe about her beauty which pulled me at once; she was not merely pretty, like the girls we regularly ogled at the Mall. Her hair was pulled back from her face into two tight braids which were rolled over her forehead. She had a perfect neck, long and elegant, not in the least scrawny, and a way of peering inquisitively forward that at once alerted me that she was related by blood to Hiranand Headmaster.

Although I was already studying for the intermediate, I regressed immediately to my schoolboy best. Joining my palms in an obsequious namaskar, I flashed her the charming sideways smile I had been practicing at home for some time for just such a chance encounter.

'Hello,' I said in English, 'Myself Mukul Nainwal.' (I had not mastered all the niceties of grammar then.) 'I am a student of Hiranand Joshi. Almost a family member, you could say. And your good self?'

I had paused delicately, shifting my balance entirely to my left leg, loping by the doorway and flashing her another Dev Anand smile. I wondered whether to extend my hand (the right one) for a friendly handshake, but quickly decided against such daring advances.

'I'm Parvati,' she had replied in Hindi, and without elaborating any further disappeared into the smoky kitchen. I had stared at her retreating figure, then groped my way through the unlit hallway into Hiranand Headmaster's study, blinded by her beauty.

'My niece Parvati will be living with me now,' he had said, sniffing elegantly at his fingernails. 'She has been studying in Jeolikote. I am her guardian now. I intend to get her married soon, it is my responsibility to my dead sister to see to that.' He had looked at me significantly, I thought, before pursing his lips into the familiar half-sneer.

I met her again the very next day. She was wearing a yellow sari. Lalit and I had been skating at the rink and I was still dizzy from the number eight I was attempting. The five o'clock siren sounded through the hills, and the setting sun stopped just to the left of China Peak. Parvati stood bathed in the last of the evening light, her saffron sari burning my soul, until my head began swimming from all the figure eights and the indescribable ecstasies of first love. At the bandstand the twenty-eight piece Kumaon regimental band began playing a snappy version of 'Bedu Pako'. Parvati was talking to a friend. In the middle of the conversation the two braids that met at her forehead came undone and tumbled down to her shoulders.

Something happened to me then. I could not move, it

was an effort even to breathe, and my eyes hungrily drank in the deep yellow of her sari till I was actually intoxicated by the colour. My best friend Lalit, my confidant, my Aziz, with whom I had until that instant been one in body and soul, nudged me to get moving. Parvati strolled over to where the two of us were standing.

'So, Mukul Nainwalji,' she said, her slim face breaking into a delicious wide grin, 'eating the fresh evening air, are you?' And indeed my mouth was agape in a most conspicuous way. Her companion giggled, and before I could articulate a reply, or even compose my reflexes to snap my mouth shut, they had both disappeared in the direction of the Naina Devi temple.

Lalit, impervious to the lightning that had struck, still innocent of the awful powers of the sisters of Eve, asked me who she was. I was tongue-tied, I could not reply, then suddenly the terrible silence released me and I was consumed by a heliotrope mirth. I slapped Lalit on the thigh, and burst into boyish hilarity, laughing until the tears began coursing down my cheeks.

Lalit, however, was more worried about an errand he had to run for Hiranand Headmaster (for he too was one of the chosen) and hurried me to the municipal library and to Royal Pharmacy thereon. It was the month of September, and everywhere flowers were in bloom. Everytime we passed a patch of yellow marigolds my heart would soar and my spirit rush out of the confines of my skin. I would look with jealous eyes at the orange marigolds, for they were not the colour of her sari, and search with tender devotion for the yellow variety. This ecstasy continued until the next time I met her. She was in a green sari now, and what with the green of the lake, and the green of the trees, and the omnipresent green paint on the doors and roofs and flowerpots of Nainital, I shifted the focus of my love to her skin, which, I decided anew, was the exact shade and texture of a young magnolia bloom.

Lalit was slow to notice my change in allegiance. We continued our evening promenades on the Mall, he discussing first-day covers or a letter from Poland he had intercepted at the post office, me staring bemusedly at the magnolia tree in bloom beside the municipal library.

I would be thinking of her still at the library counter, watching the waters of the lake and the ducks sailing by, while the librarian laboriously stamped all the volumes of Dr Freud that Hiranand Headmaster would dutifully peruse all the long night through.

I would be thinking of Parvati as we climbed up to Wee Nooke, and as Lalit knocked on the door I would quickly place multiple bets with myself about what she might be wearing. I vowed to be truthful if she was in green, charitable if she was in yellow, observe brahmacharya if she wore red.

I would be thinking of her still as Lalit and I sat in Hiranand Headmaster's study, discussing the death of Stalin, and she would enter with the tea tray. She never joined us for tea, but simply left the three teacups and the plate of Marie biscuits on his table, next to the school reports and copybooks and the softly ticking clock.

I would leave Lalit and Hiranand Headmaster to their discussions and follow her into the kitchen. Munnibee, the Muslim factotum who lived in the biwikhana, was seldom to be seen now. Parvati was scrupulous about kitchen rules and would only work barefoot, even in winter. She had marked out a chowk within which no shoes were permitted. I would stand outside the low brick demarcation and help her peel vegetables. Sometimes Munni would peep in through the window. 'Do you need any help, beti?' she would enquire in cultured Urdu.

'No Munnibee, not just now,' Parvati would reply in dulcet tones, then stick her tongue out at Munni's retreating figure.

Once, when she pulled out her tongue, I lost control. It was such a pretty tongue, so pink and clean and long. Alarmed at what I was doing, aware of the consequences, I reached out for it. Laughing, Parvati bit at my finger, drawing blood with her sharp white teeth. Tears welled up in my eyes, not of pain but of joy.

She was afraid when she saw the blood, and my finger dripping like a tap. I wiped the blood from her lips with my other hand, and felt the soft red resilience of her mouth. I let one finger linger there.

'Bite me again,' I said. She looked at me quietly, then bit me so hard that I screamed with pain. She seemed not to notice, and bit me once again with unnatural force. I was crying by now, although she drew no blood this time. My index finger was serrated by two sharp sets of tooth marks. The pain she caused made that moment almost unbearably intimate and I began to tremble.

'My engagement ring,' I told her foolishly. I had touched her lips, and read about passion.

She became instantly solicitious, and produced scissors and bandages and salt water. Both my fingers were bandaged with comically large turbans. Then, very gently, she kissed my palms, and I was poised to kiss her on the lips when

Lalit walked into the kitchen. He must have been blind not to have noticed anything; my love clung to the atmosphere as physically as did the cobwebs to the low-timbered roof. He didn't even notice my bandaged fingers.

'Hiranandji is looking for you,' he said to Parvati in a friendly, offhand sort of way. It was only after she left that he noticed the bandages.

'I say, what's up?' he asked.

'I burnt my fingers with the chimta,' I said hastily, pointing towards the blackened kitchen tongs. There was no way he could get the truth out of them.

It was only many days later that I conjured up the courage to ask her to a film. My heart thumped with guilt even in the act of buying the tickets, and I was perspiring with shame and anticipation when I handed Parvati the tickets in the kitchen. 'Let's see a film together,' I said uncertainly.

'Yes, let's,' she said matter-of-factly, chopping the green okra stems steadily as she spoke. 'Where shall we meet?'

I was primed for persuasion, so her forwardness shocked me. I handed over one ticket. 'Meet me in the hall,' I said and loped off towards Hiranand Headmaster's study, where I sat with him and Lalit and listened to the radiogram.

I remember waiting for her in the dark of the cinema hall. She came dressed in a rustly cotton sari, and without a word of greeting settled herself comfortably to watch the film, as though she were alone and unescorted.

Naturally I couldn't concentrate on the film. The light from the flickering black-and-white screen reflected on her earnest watching face. My body hungered for proximity: I was an iron filing resisting a magnet, a hurled rock defying gravity. Something in the film had made Parvati weep, tears were streaking her face like snail tracks on cement. She fumbled in her purse for a handkerchief, and her arm knocked against mine. I stopped breathing for fear she might notice that we were touching. My stomach felt as though it had been through a wringer. When she moved away I breathed again, and felt relieved as though at the end of some great ordeal.

When we left the hall it was raining outside. I was equipped with an umbrella and insisted on walking her home. It was an enormous black umbrella, and we maintained a respectable distance from each other as we plodded up towards Wee Nooke. Halfway through I saw a familiar pair of trousers under an equally familiar umbrella advancing towards us at a ferocious pace. Parvati saw him too, but we could not hide, there was nothing to do but pull the umbrella a little closer over our faces.

Hiranand Headmaster was wearing gumboots and murmuring to himself, he did not notice us at all. That night I had a wet dream, and my nightfall spattered the grimy bedsheets which my mother fortunately never bothered to change.

I had never slept with any woman, and had only the haziest notions about the anatomy of the heterosexual act. I spent all my time fantasizing about Parvati's private parts. When I met her face-to-face I would die of shame at my own dirty mind.

When Hiranand Headmaster got her married to Lalit, I saw in it a strange justice, and decided to forswear sex forever.

Adeleine was the first woman with whom I ever fornicated. You could say that she seduced me, one lonely night in Oslo, when she was newly widowed and determined to provide for her daughter. Adeleine was grieving still, and our mating was a solemn and joyless event. I had known even before ejaculating that I must propose to her.

Adeleine is a very level-headed woman, with a strong sense of order and propriety. She taught me the merits of dull comfort over passion, and gradually I was able to forget Parvati. I wrote to Hiranand Headmaster occasionally, but neither of us mentioned his niece. I was informed of Lalit's death, but knew nothing of Parvati's insanity before that last letter from my old headmaster.

I had always known, of course, that Parvati was prone to depression: her playful gaiety alternated frequently with long, silent spells, when her eyes would darken and take on an even more terrifying beauty than when she was happy. I could remember her sitting in the garden till the shadows lengthened, staring at her palms. I used to timidly try to cajole her out of the inwardness. She would extend a white hand, and point dolorously at the plunging head line. The palmistry books which were so popular then construed this as a sure sign of imminent insanity.

One summer afternoon, as I held her soft, cool palm in eager analysis, I had tactlessly repeated the observation. Her eyes had dilated with an indescribable panic.

'Don't be silly,' she said sharply and strode into the house. She returned soon after with a well-thumbed palmistry book. 'This book doesn't say anything of the sort,' she said fiercely, then, as I put my hand out to take the book from her, she laughed, 'Look at your hands, Mukul! Just look at them!'

And indeed I have small, elegant hands.

'The Inquisitors of Old Spain were men with thin hands

and pointed fingers,' she read aloud, smiling strangely. I was immensely flattered, construing it as but a reaffirmation of our love.

When I knew that she was to be married to Lalit, that her calm even-featured beauty would be his to ravage for life, I trembled violently with a terrible inward rage. I was ill for many months, telling myself that he had a murderer's hands.

Of course, he did not. No one, I think, knew that better than I. No one other than Parvati, perhaps. He was a short, muscular youth with sad eyes, a bump on his nose and a carpenter's gentle, reliable hands. He could have been a monk. He had been my only friend. I had known and loved him. He died at thirty-six of abdominal tuberculosis. Parvati had cracked up and was consigned to an asylum.

Mental illness runs like a secret rivulet through the genetic pools of Kumaon. No one is secure from its visitations. From where could Parvati have got that plunging line in her palm? Could it have been her father's sister, who came from Dubkia, and was kept chained in a cowshed until she died? Or was it from the maternal side of her family? Pooran Paper's mother was known on occasion to have walked upon her hands halfway down the Mall Road. Even Hiranand Headmaster's bitterness was indicative of some deeper inner malady. How often he had instructed me to walk down to the municipal library to borrow and return, volume by volume, the author he referred to, quite unhumorously, as Dr Sigmund Fruit. I, too, had read those volumes of Dr Fruit. Many years later, when I was still lonely and dreaming of Parvati, I had tossed and turned and clutched at my pillow, diagnosing, dissecting, distorting the loves and hatreds of my youth.

Hiranand Headmaster had loved to discuss schizophrenia. 'This entire town, for example, is schizophrenic. It has an off season personality, and another exterior one that it flaunts to the tourists. We all despise the postcards, and the people who buy them, but who doesn't want to rent out rooms to the summer-walas? We allow ourselves to be raped and prostituted every season, and then complain of lesions and rashes!' From schizophrenia to venereal disease was a sweeping diagnosis, but Hiranand Headmaster had always been partial to grand generalizations.

*

Mohan Mischief gave me to understand that Parvati's widowhood and breakdown had met with no compassion. 'She was abandoned, Mukul. She was in bad shape and no one wanted to have anything to do with her suffering,' he said with such sadness that I wanted to put an arm around his shoulder. Fed up of her brooding presence and increasingly slovenly housekeeping, Hiranand Headmaster had sent Parvati off to live with Lalit's family. But the economic burden of a widow and her child had been too much for them, and she was dispatched to the asylum at Bareilly.

Sohan Selfish looked up from his plate of dal-bhat and said fiercely, 'They even pocketed the fifty-rupee reward for turning a lunatic in!'

It was only after Hiranand Headmaster's death that a strange alliance had been established between Pooran Paper and Pushpendra. However, Mohan Mischief had hinted, his bushy eyebrows arched in insinuation, after all, there was not much those two characters could have in common besides self-interest, was there?

By the time dinner was over, my head was reeling. Mohan and Jeewan saw me to my room, and even helped me into bed. I felt rather like one of those characters in cheap spy novels who are briefed intensively for a day and a half before embarking upon a hazardous mission in a foreign culture. I longed for my wife, our flat, the Chinese-laundry smell of the bedlinen.

That night, for the first time in many years, I did not dream of Nainital. Yet the contemptuous face of the Dotyal, as he spat upon the roadside, materialized for some reason in a New York subway, where I was eyeing an ageing Mexican woman with lust.

IN ARTICULO MORTIS

My visit to the solicitor regarding Hiranandji's will was already long overdue. I decided not to delay the matter any further, and shouted to Jeewan, who was strolling in the garden below, to telephone R.C. Pande and warn him of my arrival.

I looked out of the window and inhaled the clear Himalayan air. It was a fine morning, a little on the windy side. I could hear school bells ringing, and the scuffling cries of schoolchildren, followed by the musical singing of the National Anthem.

India has what is probably amongst the longest national anthems in the world. The abbreviated, recorded version, heard in panelled, carpeted interiors, sounds very different from the lusty chants of post-Independence, post-Nehru children. I found myself mouthing the words with them.

Still humming the *Jana Gana Mana*, I examined myself indulgently in the mirror. I am quite a good-looking man. In fact, in many respects I feel I have actually improved with age. I stopped wearing glasses a few years ago, when I switched to contact lenses. My sideburns have become tinged with grey, but I have no paunch. Experience has added a certain presence to my demeanour. I have slightly crooked teeth, and what I am repeatedly assured is a most charming smile.

I shaved and went through all the other rituals of a Hindu male's daily ablutions. The shower was not working, and I am no longer comfortable with a bucket and a lota. I still stubbornly persist in wearing the sacred thread, the janeyu, procuring a new one every year from a firm in Benares through the post. I am careful never to let Adeleine see me with my janeyu fitted round my ears in our over-furnished bathroom.

I decided while dressing to try out an understated paisley scarf which I had bought from Bloomingdales the last time I was in New York. But a hirsute spider had positioned itself on the wall near the dressing table and its presence unnerved me. Try as I would, I simply could not get the knot right.

I am phobic about insects. They have always terrified me. The analytically inclined woman friend with whom I once had an affair was of the opinion that this was indicative of some latent sibling rivalry, but that was clearly impossible.

I rang for the bearer. Ram Singh shuffled in, a filthy rag thrown over one shoulder. I pointed at the arachnid. Ram Singh stared back uncomprehendingly.

'Spider!' I shouted. 'Makdi! Badua!'

The spider had shrivelled up, its legs curled inwards in apprehension. Ram Singh caught it firmly between his thumb and his forefinger and hurled it out of the window into the garden below.

'It was harmless,' he smiled, showing broken teeth. 'There

is nothing it could do to hurt you.'

I knotted the scarf to my complete satisfaction, and went downstairs to find Sohan Selfish and Mohan Mischief engrossed in a game of carom. They had set up a table in the veranda, where I sat with them and had a cup of not particularly well-made coffee.

Selfish insisted on lending me his umbrella, although the sky was clear except for some wisps of cotton wool that had strayed over China Peak. Jaundice told me that he was having a pahari meal cooked especially for me. I had already had my fill of our native cuisine, and told him that I wouldn't be back in time for lunch anyway.

At the gates of Relax Inn I collided into a young man with a briefcase. Both of us went for a tumble. I got up, dusting my behind, my hands a little grazed by the fall, and restored my precarious dignity by retrieving his bag for him from behind a hydrangea shrubbery.

He was panting heavily, as though he had been running all the way up. 'Pushpendra Pande,' he gasped, extending his hand in greeting.

I introduced myself, and waited for his reaction.

He blushed a deep scarlet. He had a very young face under a shock of prematurely greying hair, and looked superior and sarcastic, if that were possible for a man who was blushing like a beetroot. There was something about the sardonic cast of his face that was intrinsically defensive; as though he foresaw ridicule and replied to it in kind before being beaten to the draw by strangers. His transparent aggression disarmed me. Besides, he was physically not unlike Parvati.

Abandoning all preliminaries of polite conversation, he

told me hurriedly that he had come because he felt responsible for safeguarding Parvati's interests. She was his cousin, he said, and even were he not a lawyer he would have felt obliged to protest the patently unfair terms of Hiranandji's will. He would, he said, do everything in his power to ensure that she got her due, even if he had to appeal all the way to the Supreme Court in the process.

I watched him curiously as he scowled his way through his ill-rehearsed spiel. Something about the set of the shoulders, and the fine, almost feminine hands, suggested his cousin as I had known her.

I said that I had nothing to gain from the will, and were it not for a purely sentimental desire to go along with Hiranandji's last wishes, I would never have got involved in the whole business.

'But what about Irra?' he demanded. 'Have you ever considered her situation? She is my niece! I would even have kept her with me, but she and my Mrs! Oil and water!'

I told him that I was fully cognisant of my responsibilities, and that I would certainly see to Irra's welfare. Perhaps I could somehow contrive to make her a beneficiary of the trust, but surely it was premature to discuss terms before I had even met with Hiranand Headmaster's solicitor.

He was about to launch into another tirade, but I stopped him in time. 'We had better meet again after I have discussed matters with the lawyer,' I said. 'Perhaps you'll cool down by then. And please telephone for an appointment next time.'

I felt I had handled the whole thing very well. Armed with Sohan's multicoloured umbrella and the triple-proof armour of self-satisfaction, I set off to meet R.C. Joshi at his chambers.

I walked briskly down the Mall Road towards Tallital. Tallital Bazaar was crowded, chaotic and clothed in the sickly sweet odour of decay. Myriads of tiny gnats, invisible to the naked eye, but lit up now by some trick of the troubled sunlight, danced over the exposed sewers. Throngs of pedestrians crowded the intersection; buses and cars and taxis collided with coolies and dandies and rickshaws.

I rechecked the address from Hiranand Headmaster's letter, which I had brought with me in a folder. R.C. Joshi and Co. were situated above Royal Pharmacy, Tallital.

Royal Pharmacy appeared Royal no longer. I sidestepped it and huffed up an almost vertical staircase to find myself upon a dark landing, where a small window opened out on yet more dilapidated habitations. Here a beautifully crafted teak door stood boarded up with strips of plywood. A penciled notice stuck on the door read: 'R.C. Joshi, B.A., L.L.B.' This was accompanied by an enigmatic penciled arrow drawn with a red felt pen. I climbed up yet more stairs, breathing the forgotten odours of asafoetida and dust.

R.C. Joshi, B.A., L.L.B., was a bit of a surprise. He did not look in the least like what I thought a lawyer ought to, for he was dressed in a conventional white shirt and a pair of flowing orange chiffon pyjamas. As if that were not unsettling enough, he began conversing with me in a disconcertingly pucca British accent.

'I say, old chap,' he chuckled, 'come into a bit of luck, haven't we? Must say, it was quite decent of the old boy to pass on all his moolah to you. What do you say, Biggles?' Biggles turned out to be a placid Bhotiya puppy, who was persuaded to come out from under the table to shake hands with me and be introduced as "Major James Bigglesworth, Esq."'

I was at a complete loss for words. When I had recovered from the shock I discovered that, apart from the orange pyjamas, there was nothing particularly aberrational about Joshi. He outlined my legal position, and gave me a lucid account of Hiranand Headmaster's finances. In addition to the properties, these were some forty thousand rupees in a post office savings account.

'Here is the testamentary disposition of his property,' he said, extracting some stamped paper from within the recesses of a meat safe which stood beside his desk. Hiranand Headmaster's will was a rambling, ill-drafted document, full of high sentence, and a bit obtuse. I examined it with clerical detachment.

'I, Hiranand Ballabh Joshi, R/o Wee Nooke, Nainital, S/o Jaydev Chand Joshi, being in full possession of my mind and faculties, do declare this to be my last Will and Testament.

'I do declare that all monies, assets and properties listed herein are entirely self-acquired, and therefore wish to ensure that a thorough medical check-up be conducted upon me to ensure and ascertain that I am de facto legally and medically no longer in possession of my Life or Senses at the time of my Demise. Furthermore that all my viscera and organs be donated to the noble cause of Science after the expiry of my last breath.'

The wherefore of the therefore eluded me. I sought elucidation from R.C. Joshi. He smiled amiably at me.

'He was a true conceptual! Of course, he was suffering from cancer of the intestines,' he said. 'But a thorough gentleman!'

I read on.

'I warn that certain Serpents I have been harbouring in my nest may choose indeed to contest the terms and conditions of my will. No credence to be given to any bills, contentions or documents such malicious individuals may subsequently produce.

'The disposal of the above-mentioned monies, movable and immovable assets and properties to be left to the sole and absolute discretion of Mukul Nainwal Esp. R/o Hong Kong (in whom I repose eternal and abiding faith), to be used for Charitable purposes concerning the perpetuation of my Life's Work, i.e. Education, and for the physical and moral upliftment of our Hill Folk.

'To all other near and dear ones I bequeath my Love and Blessings. The last rites to be conducted by dear Pooran. The ashes may be scattered to the four winds from China Peak, to spare him the expense of a journey to Rishikesh.'

There were a lot of further notes and codicils, all hammered out on an exceptionally jumpy manual typewriter. All the pages were initialled in that familiar wavering schoolmaster's hand.

''Fraid the orchard's a bit sticky, old man,' R.C. Joshi said in his strange nasal accent. 'The chowkidar Johnny's done some golmaal with the land records. Better watch out for that other bloke as well—he and that journalist chappie are hand in glove to do you out of Wee Nooke. Seems the sarkar is planning a ropeway to Snow View, and land prices are bound to skyrocket!'

As I was trying to disentangle the bloke from the chappie and the Johnny, I realized that the incongruous accent was nowhere as fluent as it had first appeared. It was a carefully rehearsed pastiche, a sham.

I could contain my curiosity no longer. 'Why the orange chiffon pyjamas, sir?' I asked as naturally as I could.

'Of course, young man,' he replied, 'but of course. The orange I wear because it is the colour of renunciation. Under the spiritual guidance of Bala Mahadev Pachisi Baba, I have long since renounced all fruits of action. The chiffon because I dislike waste, and my daughter had torn this sari and didn't know what to do with it. As for the pyjamas, I confess that is entirely a matter of convention, not rational at all. Very comfortable, these pyjamas, as it happens.'

It was an altogether rational explanation.

THE MAGNOLIA TREE

On my way down from Pande's chambers, I wandered on a stray impulse into Royal Pharmacy. I had been a frequent customer there, buying medicines for my mother, and, later, sometimes, chocolates for Parvati. It was as dusty as it had ever been; huge jars of sweets pillared the counters, and an improbable array of antiquated and quite useless goods crowded the shelves.

After much deliberation, I decided to buy Irra some bars of chocolate, and attempt the climb up to Wee Nooke. My confidence in my physical condition and powers of perambulation had risen considerably since my return.

The walk from Tallital to Snow View is longer but less steep than it is from Mallital. Crowded ill-constructed tenements had mushroomed almost all the way up. The parapets were broken, garbage and rubble lined the road. I wondered how the municipality had allowed any building activity here at all, for the mountain soil is extremely weak. Unregulated construction here is nothing short of an invitation to disaster.

I knew there was a contradiction in my thinking, that houses were really more important than landscapes. Still I found myself almost wishing that, as in the landslide of 1880, the hills would reject all this ugliness and contemptuously tip it into the lake below.

Even at this height, I would every now and then encounter sturdy Tibetan hill ponies toiling upwards, laden with bricks. Television antennae straggled from rooftops. Gradually the builders and the populace seemed to tire of the climb, and the houses gave way to forests of chir and deodar, banj and tilonj.

On my right, clothed by mist and fog, were the unseen presences of the Himalayan snow peaks. There rose Trishul, Nanda Kot and the Panchaula, where the five Pandavas had cooked their dinners in the course of their ascent to heaven. In the centre stood Naina Devi with her grey pyramidical peak, rising I think to 2,566 feet.

But there was no view today, and I would have to huff here another morning to pay my homage to the snows.

I arrived at Wee Nooke considerably the worse for wear. Irra was sitting alone in the garden, perched upon a huge boulder, her eyes glued to a pair of binoculars. Dressed in her school uniform, and in her large clumsy black shoes, she looked more like an agile species of monkey than a young girl. She sensed my presence, and clambered down from her perch.

'No school today?' I asked avuncularly, handing her the chocolates.

'Miss was ill today,' she replied, 'and there's no one at home. Shall I get you some tea?' And without waiting for a reply she went into the house, leaving me alone in the garden.

The binoculars waited on the parapet near the boulder. I adjusted them this way and that. My vision settled upon a beautiful glade of oak and cypress a little distance away. I espied bare feminine haunches; a young girl was enjoying the privacy of the grassy hollow to defecate. A bottle of water lay beside her.

I turned away, embarrassed, and wondered whether this was the view Irra had been engrossed in.

She returned with the tea. 'You will have lunch here?' she asked, and again it was more a statement than a question.

'Yes, that would be nice,' I replied, for I had nothing else to do, and this was, after all, my house now.

'Do you like Maggi Instant Noodles?' she asked hopefully.

'Anything will do,' I said accommodatingly, 'anything at all.'

The Maggi Instant Noodles were a fair success. We ate in companionable silence, and then she shared a chocolate with me.

'Would you like to rest for a while?' she asked when we had finished. 'Masterji's khaat is empty.' Little as I liked the idea of resting on the dead man's bed, I was so tired by the climb that I accepted gratefully, and followed her into the rear bedroom.

The room was like a large shoebox, with no ventilation at all, save a small skylight. Two ancient wooden beds were set parallel to each other.

'That is my bed,' Irra said, 'and that was his.' An immense golden-haired doll reclined on Hiranandji's bed. 'That's Sheela,' Irra said, 'Raju chacha sent her from Bombay. She's a walkie-talkie.' She gathered the doll in her arms and carried her out of the room, pulling the string on Sheela's back in demonstration as she departed. Peal upon peal of hysterical laughter filled the room. The vision of Sheela's cruel blonde countenance and those ghoulish paroxysms of laughter continued to torment me long after they had both left the room.

I lay there for less than half an hour. It was impossible to rest. A peculiar smell which I chose not to investigate had settled upon the mattress. I tried not to imagine Hiranand Headmaster lying there, day after day, his body enfeebled, his faculties wasting. It would have been easier if he had believed in God, if he had believed in anything.

I left without telling Irra, who was fast asleep in the next room, huddled under a quilt, one arm dangling almost to the floor. Sheela lay beside her.

In the garden, I paused under the magnolia tree. Its heady smell was familiar and disturbing. I tried not to think of Parvati, for her remembrance was now verging upon the obsessive. I walked away and a few steps later all but tumbled into a large hole which the rains had excavated into the weak soil. It was not very wide, and only a few feet deep. Through the crumbling shale I could see the exposed roots of the magnolia tree, gnarled and strong, as they spread about in search of sustenance.

*

An English friend who had lived in these parts once described Nainital as 'a sort of a Himalayan Brighton'. Indeed, it is a sort of demented pleasure palace. The perpetual frenetic gaiety of the flats was almost unbearable after the tiring walk down. I decided to seek refuge in the club, and soon I was sitting on the deck overlooking the lake, munching tomato-and-cheese sandwiches. The yachts were moored nearby, their brightly striped sails flapping uncomfortably in the breeze. I read the names upon their prows. 'Kestrel', 'Merlin', 'Molly', 'Seagull', 'Pirouette', 'Stella', 'Scout' and a lone 'Taringini'.

A rising wind slapped the green waters against the jetty. Half-eaten corn cobs and decomposing flowers dashed with the waves against the rocky shore. On the hill opposite, on the dark Ayarpatta side, birch trees shimmered and changed colour with the breeze. I decided to return to the hotel.

I cut across the flats on my way back. There was a football match in progress. Little turrets of dust rose and circled in the wind. The revelry of the Nanda Devi mela had not yet reached fever pitch. Something compelled me to seek out the young Tibetan woman. She was seated as before upon the tin trunk. There were no customers at her stall. She was dressed in the same black baku. A green ribbon was plaited into her lustrous black hair.

Again I was overcome by the same uncontrollable lust. I wanted her more than I had ever wanted any woman before. I looked hungrily at the moist red mouth. She had large white teeth and an aureate golden skin. Small gold hoops intertwined with red thread hung from her tiny ears.

Pretending not to have noticed me, she picked up a ball of wool which lay beside her and busied herself in unhurried knitting. A mischievous smile, which she tried ineffectually to hide, played about her face.

I bent down and fingered a small silver snuff box crudely encrusted with lapis lazuli. 'How much for this?' I enquired. Her eyes met mine. I was breathing in short quick gasps. At this psychological moment I felt the pressure of a friendly hand pounding fiercely upon my back. I almost choked, and turned guiltily around to find none other than the excitable Rakesh Kumar, alone, bereft of Ramlala and Prithipal Singh.

He was chewing on a paan. His lips and teeth were stained a deep red, his mouth still set in that perpetually astonished cast.

'How much is this?' I asked her again.

'Eighty rupees,' she replied, still concentrating upon the knitting, but the smile vanished from her lips. I bought it, and paid her, and began walking back towards the hotel. Rakesh Kumar fell into step with me.

'If I modestly say, your good self should not have agreed to eighty,' he said. 'She would have brought it down to thirty. This is India, brother, not advanced country like the Hong Kong. You are too good for this world.' He spat out the paan, sloshing it about my shoes. I directed a murderous look at him. My displeasure must have conveyed itself to him, for he said hastily that he had better be going.

By the time I returned to the hotel I was completely exhausted. I collapsed into bed and lay there for a long time. It was dark outside. Ram Singh came and switched on the light, and made the bed for the night.

I told him I would like dinner in the room. He asked concernedly if I was feeling all right, and brought up a heap of old magazines for me to read.

Someone had attempted to brighten up my room with a vase of tightly packed dahlias. The dangling cord of the light bulb in its dusty bamboo shade swayed in rhythm to unknown air currents, like some misshapen pendulum. There were violent fluctuations in the voltage, and the table lamp did not appear to be in working condition. I consoled myself with an excess of duty-free whisky, and leafed through the disintegrating volumes of Atkinson's *Himalayan Gazetteer*, which I had rescued from Hiranand Headmaster's library.

My eyes focused with some difficulty upon the yellowing paper and the fine serif typeface. 'Of the Honesty of the Hill People,' I read, 'too much praise cannot be given. Property of every kind is left exposed without fear and without loss. Of the inhabitants, everyone speaks well. They are indeed dirty to a degree I have never seen among the Hindoos, and extremely averse to any improvement in their rude and inefficient agriculture, but they are honest, peaceable and cheerful...'

While appreciating the perspicacious sociological insight of our departed rulers I was sick to my teeth of 'our honest hill folk'. I retired to my dressing room to change into my pyjamas only to discover that my spider, or another that resembled it inordinately, had returned to its post beside the mirror. I spent a tortured night, for my legs ached in all the most unreasonable places, and I was kept awake until dawn by the distracting laughter and constantly creaking beds in the room next to mine.

PASANG RAMPA

I t is not always easy to tell the truth. Every life has its reluctant secrets. It was almost as though I were fated to meet the Tibetan girl again. In retrospect I cannot understand my behaviour with her, or why I went to her room at all.

The day after, though, I did sit down and clinically analysed all the elements that compounded her attractions.

a)   I was extremely lonely.

b)   She was, in face and figure, my 'type'. She had the unmistakable peculiarities of feature that belong to the Mongolian race.

c)   The encounter had all the elements of surreptitiousness and danger that I associate with certain houses of easy virtue in Kowloon side.

d)   I am an incurable romantic.

As a student of history I believe that every event has an immediate and a historic cause. In this case the immediate cause was that my physical desires were getting out of hand (no pun intended).

I had encountered her again, after Rakesh Kumar's rude

interruption, in Malli Bazaar. I was browsing through books and magazines at Consul Book Depot. I had not slept well the previous night, and felt out of sorts with myself and the world. Here in the bookshop, surrounded by words and print and paper, I was somehow reassured. I bought a copy of the *Far Eastern Economic Review*, and even an out of date *Asiaweek*.

I literally bumped into her as I stepped out. She smiled at me invitingly. She was dressed in a dark-blue baku, underneath which she wore a striped rugby sweater. She had on high-heeled sandals and was carrying some incomplete knitting in a plastic bag. She looked captivating. Desperate for any ploy, I asked her if Rakesh Kumar's allegations about her overpricing had any truth in them.

She was suitably outraged. 'Come to my room just now!' she said, in surprisingly good English. 'Come to my room and see for yourself the manufacturers' rate-cards! We Tibetans do not cheat anybody!'

Her cheeks were flushed with anger, and her delectable lips somehow fuller than I remembered. She bit at them in chagrin. She had even, white teeth. I watched bemused.

I had found myself agreeing. 'Let's go,' I told her, 'I would like to see those rate-cards.' She was a little taken aback. I noticed a fine film of sweat upon her upper lip.

Tibet had always been a forbidden country. When I was a boy I had sometimes encountered strangely-dressed Bhotiyas who traded in salt and borax; they stank of yak butter and told tales of gold-panning on the Sona river. My mother warned me not to talk to them. She was certain that they would kidnap me.

'I live nearby,' the Tibetan girl said. 'Come with me.' She

was still very angry. She turned away without waiting for me and began walking rapidly uphill, her high-heeled sandals clicking like angry knitting needles on the cobbled street. I followed a little way behind, lest anyone think I was walking with her.

'I live upstairs,' she said, pointing her striped-sweatered arm at the rickety wooden staircase by the side of the two-storeyed building. It was a bravely cheerful compound. Its inhabitants did not appear in the least intimidated by poverty. Flowers bloomed in profusion. A red-cheeked child was clambering up an apricot tree. Everything seemed orderly and happy. I was embarrassed, and felt like an intruder.

'Upstairs,' she said, and led me up the staircase. I trod warily, one step at a time, holding on uneasily to the handrail, my heart missing a beat with every shaky step.

The entrance to her room was chained and padlocked. She produced a key from somewhere within the folds of her baku and soundlessly unlocked the door. It was extremely dark inside. I searched for a light but could find none. She opened a little window by the bed. Daylight streamed in.

Behind the window I could see a steep mountain wall, reinforced by crumbling bricks, resplendent with rich green moss and maidenhair.

The Tibetan girl opened a tin trunk and began fumbling agitatedly through it. She finally found what she wanted, and handed me a brightly printed rate-card. The trunk was overflowing with trinkets and variously coloured woollen shawls.

'Look at this price list! I have not cheated you! We buy directly from the wholesalers in Ludhiana. My old mother, she sells these shawls. She is in Chandigarh now.'

A Tibetan Tankha painting, shrouded in yellowing veils, hung on one wall. A pair of blue jeans were slung from a nail on another.

I scrutinized the price list. I didn't quite know how to respond. 'I am sorry. I was wrong. I believe you now,' I said.

We sat in silence. 'Tell me about yourself,' I said.

She looked me straight in the eyes. 'I have a passport,' she whispered. 'I am a Tibetan girl. My name is Pasang Rampa. I am well educated. Somebody told me you are from Hong Kong. I want a visa to live in Hong Kong.'

'What sort of a passport,' I asked, slightly taken aback by her directness.

'It is an Indian passport,' she replied proudly.

'Then in that case you don't really need a visa to go to Hong Kong,' I said helplessly.

She was staring at me.

I checked furtively to ensure that the door was locked. Her eyes followed my gaze.

'Tell me about yourself,' I said again.

'My name is Pasang Rampa,' she replied. The expression on her face was impassive. 'My family, they came from Tibet, from the U Tsang province. We had a house near Lhasa. Then the Chinese, they came. The Dalai Lama came to India. My family, they fled in terror. I studied in India. I have one sister. We went to boarding school in Dharamasala. My sister, she works in a Chinese restaurant in Chandigarh.'

I listened politely. 'My old mother, she is in Chandigarh just now. She came from a very big family. She talks a lot about life in Tibet. Not that I pay much attention to her stories. Those days are in the past!' She seemed to need to go on talking.

'My boyfriend, he is Christian. He is going to marry me. My old mother, she is very old-fashioned.'

She searched in the fold of her baku before producing another key, then opened a creaky trunk and began rummaging through it. She extracted an exquisite necklace fashioned of jade and turquoise worked with fine seed pearls and held it out for me to see.

'My mother brought it with her when they fled from Tibet. My parents were not poor like you see us now. In Tibet they lived in a proper house and did not work. Then the Chinese, they attacked Tibet, and the Dalai Lama, he fled to India. Now we are poor and homeless. I don't mind but...'

I had heard it all before. It was the familiar litany of refugees and displaced people the world over.

I looked at Pasang Rampa. She looked sad and beautiful. She smelt of sweat and cheap talcum powder. The two were somehow compounded into the scent of magnolias.

I looked around at the room. The mud floor had been freshly swabbed, and was covered with a bright Tibetan rug. A small wooden table held a petromax lamp and a half-melted candle shaped like the Venus De Milo.

Now she was ferreting through yet another trunk, from which she produced a small jade box. 'For you, a present,' she said, placing it in the palm of my hand. 'We Tibetans, we do not cheat anybody. Now I will get you some tea.'

I was stricken, shamed by her generosity. She unlocked the door and went to the adjoining room to make tea. She returned carrying an aluminium tray which contained two expensive China cups.

'How did you know that I come from Hong Kong?' I asked.

'Your friend, he told me,' she said. 'That man you were talking to. But that was not why...' Then she was quiet and handed me my tea.

'I like Nainital,' she continued, 'but there is nothing that I can do here. I do not want to sell shawls and scent bottles all my life! Is there work to do in Hong Kong? My boyfriend, he is very clever.'

'Hong Kong reverts to China soon,' I said.

'The Chinese,' she said reflectively.

I gave her my card. 'Give me another,' she said, and wrote her name upon it with a straggly hand. I wondered about the address but didn't ask.

Back in my room, I listed out the five most beautiful women in the world.

1. Elizabeth Taylor (when she was younger)
2. Madhubala
3. The Maharani of Jaipur
4. Ratna Dewi Sukarno
5. Parvati, when she had been young

A NEW ARRIVAL

One morning I found myself abandoned by the three brothers. Sohan, Mohan and Jeewan were all fussing importantly over the vacant corner table to my right.

A honeymooning couple was breakfasting at the table to my left, the woman wearing a great deal of gold jewellery for that time of the morning, and the constipated sleepless look distinctive to diligent newly-weds. The male looked withered and humiliated.

The corner table, as yet unoccupied, was being readied, as it were, for royalty. Relax Inn had risen to a clean table-cloth with clean napkins and an almost-clean waiter to match.

Jeewan Jaundice inartistically crammed a fat bunch of drooping mauve dahlias into an old porcelain vase. Sohan Selfish conducted an operational check upon the matching salt and pepper pots and spattered their contents over the fresh table-cloth, necessitating it to be reversed. Mohan scurried about bearing armloads of chutneys and jams and vitamin tablets, which he deposited on the antipodal fabric.

Water spilled over from the crowded vase onto the table-cloth, and all three began trading accusations and having little tantrums until a bearer brought in more freshly laundered linen. He pacified each of them individually, smoothing the creases, wiping the vase and arranging the chutney and vitamin-pill bottles in a neat circular arrangement.

Suddenly the brothers scampered to distant corners of the dining hall. The honeymooners were gaping at the entrance, transfixed by some emotion I could not identify. The man looked more abject than ever before. His wife sprinted out of the hall. I could hear her thumping all the way up the stairs.

A person with an unnaturally pink complexion swaggered in and settled himself easily at the special table. A sullen-looking woman in a dressing gown trailed in after him. I was fascinated by the man's colouring. He seemed by some accident of pigmentation to have acquired the exact tint of healthy raw flesh. He wore pointed white snakeskin shoes. His clothes were otherwise European high street. I decided that he must be a film star.

The honeymooning woman returned waving an autograph book. The three brothers assembled around my table to announce that the pink man was none other than The Film Star Jayesh and his Mrs.

I displayed polite interest. Secretly I was resentful that no one had thought of changing the linen or placing dahlias at my table.

I retreated to my room to sulk. Leafing through the old issues of the *Illustrated Weekly* which Ram Singh had brought up for me, I discovered that the magazine had discontinued carrying the wedding photographs of selected readers, which I remembered as being one of its most popular features. I had always followed the details of these unions with unfailing interest. They were crammed into the penultimate pages of the magazine, next to the classified advertisements for remedies for White Spots and Venereal Disease and Loss of Vigour in Married Life. A mugshot photograph of Parvati and myself, with a published announcement regarding our nuptials, had then appeared to be the unattainable and yet inevitable culmination of all the aspirations of my adolescence.

Turning the pages I came upon an article featuring Jayesh. A coloured photograph showed him dressed in pink leotards and pointed white shoes. 'I am bored of being a hero,' he said. I could not help reading on.

'Nobody can grudge me the millions I make,' the article began. 'There is no doubt that I am Number Two. It was not an easy climb to the top. If I am where I am today it is all due to the grace of God.'

I flipped the page: 'Your Luck This Week'. A vestigial faith in horoscopes, fortune cookies, *I Ching* and computer printouts still lurks in my rational mind. I believe in signs and portents and constantly analyse my dreams. I am a Cancerian. My birthday falls on the twenty-fifth of June. My forecast for a week long gone read: 'Members of the Armed Forces, Fire Fighting Services and Police may earn honours for their devotion to duty. If you are an industrialist, with a range of interests, profits will increase. If eligible, you are likely to marry a childhood friend. The married will experience a phase of stability. A dispute regarding ancestral property will be resolved. Avoid hasty decisions. Take care of your health. You must display courage in the face of physical danger.' It sounded excessive to me—improbable in the context of my present life, at least. No time in my recent past has ever seemed so full of possibility as this horoscope promised. Would it have been different if Parvati had been mine, if I had stayed on in these hills? I am fairly sure not; and yet it seems sometimes that I live a life diminished by loss and exile.

A centipede was crawling with slow deliberation across the arm of my chair, advancing towards me. I displayed more physical courage than I have done at various critical junctures of my life. Tearing a page out of the *Weekly* I crumpled the hapless creature into it, and hurled the paper into the garden below. Then I washed my hands in the hygienic tiled bathroom, where a burly spider had slung out its web by the sink.

I decided to rearrange my clothes, and stacked the shirts and underwear methodically on the shelves. My trousers and suits swung like skeletons on the other side of the cavernous cupboard.

Tired by these exertions, I lay down in bed for a pre-lunch siesta, and indulged in a pleasant reverie about Pasang Rampa. The exasperating creak-thump-creak resumed from next door.

At lunch time, the mood and menu had switched to Raj Nouvelle. We were served a sweetish almond soup and mutton cutlets and custard. Jayesh's wife was still in her dressing gown.

All of us, including Jayesh and his wife, sat in the veranda after lunch. The cleanest of the waiters brought out a basket of fruit. It was drizzling slightly. A soft fog was stealthily swallowing the garden.

Jayesh was extremely forthcoming about his private life. He seemed to be under the impression that he was being interviewed. In a short while I knew more about him than I do about most of my intimate friends and relatives, Adeleine included. He insisted upon calling me Professor, which somehow pleased me.

In short:

a)   His last film had not flopped at the box office.

b)   His wife Anita was 'very understanding', and they had no marital problems whatsoever.

c)   He was not having an affair with Sundari.

d)   The new crop of heroines were very professional.

e)   There is nothing worse for health than constipation.

f)   His son had not been expelled from Sherwood College.

g)   He had never had a facelift.

h)   He knew Run Shaw and Jimmy Carter.

i)   He knew the Prime Minister of India.

j)   He thought film stars should not interfere in politics.

k)   He had studied in Sherwood College himself, and didn't know why the principal was being so hard on his son.

l)   He was a man of the soil, and not like a film star at all.

m)   He bought his clothes in Paris, never in Hong Kong.

n)   His wife understood him perfectly.

o)   He had not entered into a bigamous marriage with Sundari.

At this stage my mind began to wander, although the brothers were still listening spellbound. Anita had peeled and consumed all the oranges. Peel and rind and orange pips lay scattered at her feet as though in homage to her understanding. She looked sullen and knowing.

Jayesh instantly sensed my loss of interest, which must have offended his performer's instincts, for he set about conjuring a change in atmosphere.

'Let me tell you about my trip to Hong Kong, Professor,' he wheedled, and enacted what seemed to me an improbable tale about a dinner party where the main course of live monkey brain had dashed out of the dining table into the casinos.

I had heard many such stories of culinary parochialism, and was more than a little bored by them. But Jayesh was determined to raise a laugh from me. He looked me in the eyes, and, smiling a crooked charming smile, locked me into inexorable eye contact.

Then he rose to this feet and began gyrating to a nimble, comical folk dance such as hill people perform at festivals and fairs.

Bedu pako
Baramasa
Oho Kaphal pako Chaita,
Meri Chhaila
Tyera Khuta
Kanta bud lo
Mera khuta peeda,
Meri Chhaila.

He had even extracted a Hermes scarf from somewhere, which he twirled and angled at us in happy abandon.

Mohan joined in the dance as well, and Jeewan, Sohan and I began clapping in time with the song. When they finally stopped, laughing and breathless, Jayesh flashed me a triumphant smile. 'I am just a simple hill boy at heart, Professor,' he said. 'A Delhi-wala by birth but my heart belongs to these hills.' He was clutching at his heart as he spoke.

He tried to explain the song to his wife. 'It's a love song, darling,' he told her. Then he gave up.

'My wife is a Sindhi,' he sighed. 'She can never understand.'

'Such simple people, Professor,' he exclaimed again. His monogrammed shirt pocket was crumpled where he had been clutching at his heart. 'Nobody in these hills ever locked their houses, fifty years ago. Or their hearts, even now. I employ only Pahari servants in Bombay. Even my hairdresser Sher Singh is a Pahari, yaar.'

We got to talking about my inheritance, and the uses it could be put to. Soon, a picnic was planned to the orchard near Bhowali. Jayesh wanted to take his son on the excursion. I decided to take Irra as my guide. The three brothers volunteered their company as well. Jayesh had two cars, so the logistics were looked after. We would all go the very next day, Jayesh decided enthusiastically.

*

Pooran Paper came to see me in the evening. He had a bad cold. His eyes were a strange red colour and he had a very runny nose.

He touched my feet and murmured a respectful '*pai lago*' upon entering the room. I shuffled aside, embarrassed.

Nothing in our relationship warranted this traditional greeting; besides he had merely shaken hands with me on our two previous meetings.

'I just don't know what to say, Mukul daju,' he said abjectly. His voice was hoarse as the sighing of pines. 'I have paid the deposit for a flat in a building which Satish Sah Ji is constructing; I have managed to arrange the money somehow. But it will take at least three more months to complete. I was hoping you would let me stay on till then.'

He took out several crumpled tissues from his pocket and wiped his nose with all of them at once. 'I don't know what to do, where to go,' he snivelled pathetically.

I began feeling sorry for him. It was decent of him to ask me, for I was not really in a position to evict him from Wee Nooke.

'Of course you can stay,' I said magnanimously, 'stay as long as you like, Pooran. After all, I am not inhuman.'

'I shall never forget this generosity, Mukul daju!' he replied, wiping his nose upon the sleeve of his sweater.

It appeared that he wanted to interview me for his newsletter. He would come again with a photographer, he said, and gave me a questionnaire so that I could answer at leisure.

I told him about our proposed visit to Bhowali, and of my intention to take Irra with me. We discussed Wee Nooke again. He was of the opinion that it could be converted into a centre for ecological studies, with Pooran himself as the director-in-charge. Before leaving he presented me with a brown-paper bundle, which proved upon inspection to contain back issues of the *Himalayan Times*, the periodical which he edited.

Pooran blew his nose again, and sneezed several times in succession. Yet more tissues materialized. All of them looked soggy and ineffectual. He strolled over to the window and, leaning out, blew his nose hard, tapping and probing his proboscis delicately with his forefinger in the time-honoured Pahari fashion. For someone so ecologically minded, he was remarkably uninhibited in the disposal of olfactory waste.

To my horror, he touched my feet again as he left, promising as he left to send Irra to Relax Inn by nine the next morning, in time for our excursion to Bhowali.

APPLES AND ORANGES

I awoke to discover that the passage downstairs was littered with multicoloured plastic mugs and tubs and basins, all strategically placed as catchments for the leaking roof.

Irra was waiting for me downstairs. She was seated in the veranda, tense but self-contained. She was dressed in what had obviously once been a man's trousers. They had been inexpertly altered, and were of a strange material and texture. The bump on her nose seemed more prominent than ever.

Jayesh's son had not been allowed leave from his school. The brothers said that they could not come either, as a tin slat from the kitchen roof had flown off the night before and had to be repaired. Besides, a large overnight party was expected from Ranikhet, and rooms had to be readied for them.

That left only Jayesh and his wife, and Irra and myself. Anita hadn't dressed, she was still in her dressing gown. She said she had a headache. Jayesh was a film star and couldn't go alone, so Jeewan offered to go in her stead. We decided to take only one car.

Jeewan sat in front with the driver, and Irra settled down between Jayesh and me. Irra put on quite a different face in company. She was poised and aloof, and her manners could not be faulted. Jayesh seemed a genuinely uncomplicated person. He asked her who her favourite film star was, but she would not reply.

'Tell me who he is, don't be shy,' he said jocularly. He poked her in the ribs and gave me a broad wink.

Irra's lips set in a thin line of reproof. 'I do not watch films and I do not admire film stars,' she said primly. I was proud for her precarious young snootiness, her fragile pride.

Jayesh also eyed her with a certain surprise. 'People in small towns are usually star-struck,' he shrugged.

We drove past the municipal library, the Alka, Everest, and India hotels, and the church of St. Francis on to a road that clung nervously to the mountainside. The monsoon fog engulfed us. Grey and sure-footed, it crept about the pines, sometimes parting to reveal the brooding profile of the hills.

Every here and there we would encounter an uprooted tree. Our hills are not very strong, and the weak soil can barely withstand the onslaught of the rains. The road to Bhowali was littered with minor landslides. Despite the rain, gangs of workmen were labouring to repair the damage.

Swollen mountain streams flowed down in torrential cascades. Banks of cloud floated and collided and reformed, and we could see the wind lashing the rain into patterns on the other side of the hill. Jeewan produced some apples from a bag and passed them around. They were a mottled green-red colour, not the standard produce of supermarkets. We munched contentedly.

'Do you know,' Jayesh said, 'if I wasn't up to my ears in

debt, I would give up everything, every film I have on hand, my house and my flat in Bombay, even my wife perhaps, though not my son, and come and live up here in the hills.'

Irra's eyes glimmered with contempt.

'This is where I grew up,' Jayesh continued, 'and this is where I would like to die. Among simple people, and goodness and beauty.' I was touched by his sincerity. Jeewan turned back from the front seat and looked at us earnestly.

'The hills are not the same any more,' he said. 'People want all sorts of things now. They watch television, and they want Surf and Lux and Colgate. But you can't use detergents and cosmetics when you go to the riverside to bathe! The men go off to the plains to find work and leave their women here in the hills to plough the fields. When they come back to harvest, their wives have had yet another baby, from where or how no one is ever sure. Oh, our hills are becoming just like the plains! They come here to escape the summer heat and leave their city habits behind! Every summer our temples are robbed! We Paharis are simple folk, we are not greedy! It's as though we enjoyed being poor!' he concluded bitterly. It was the longest speech I had ever heard Jeewan make.

Jayesh turned to me. 'You have the chance of a lifetime, Professor,' he said. 'With your contacts, you could get all sorts of assistance and grants. I could help you collect money as well. You could so something. Educate them. Help them.'

His excitement was infectious, but I knew there was nothing I could do. I could not pipe water, nor make the soil fertile; I could not create industries, or jobs, or even grants and quotas. All I could do was help a few more to run away, as Hiranand Headmaster had helped me. Or I could run back myself, and shelter in the pride of destitution, the acceptance of sorrow, the banishment of ambition. I could shed my worries about credit cards and boring dinner parties, but very little else. I could build a house, plant a tree. It was too late now to have a son.

I had never been to the orchard before. Hiranandji had bought it upon his retirement, and left it in the charge of a Thakur from his village. We located it without much difficulty. It was some fifteen kilometres from Bhowali, on the Ramgarh Road. I could not see much of our surroundings because of the enveloping mist. Here or there a single pine or deodar stood out in silhouette, indicating the lay of the mountains.

The cottage was situated in a small clearing. It consisted of a covered veranda, two small rooms and a kitchen. The bathroom was a shed a little distance away, and connected to the cottage by a catwalk.

Although he had never actually lived here, Hiranand Headmaster had constantly been threatening the move. He would write to me about his plans to sell Wee Nooke, leaving Pooran and his family and Irra to fend for themselves. But of course he could never have lived here, his health would not have permitted it. The place was much too remote, and its maintenance must have been a considerable drain upon his resources. Nevertheless it had a certain cosy charm, and was, in many ways, ideal for a retired life.

The caretaker, Dan Singh, was a thin wiry man. He seemed to have kept everything in good order. I was keen to question him about the management of the orchard, but he was so overcome by the arrival of the Film Star Jayesh that he brushed me aside as though I were some odious irritant.

Dan Singh dismissed my enquiries about the orchard with a disconcerting finality. 'It's useless to talk about all that,' he said brusquely. Waving me away he began genuflecting and oleaginating before Jayesh, plying him with arcane questions about film lore.

We looked about us at the grey sky and the crabbed cringing trees, at the broken bathroom door and the unused cowsheds, and consumed the unappetizing food which Jeewan had got packed. We ate our lunch alfresco, on the bonnet of the car. Irra had an enormous appetite. She licked her fingers clean when she had finished, and let out a small, polite burp.

Dan Singh gave us two crates of pockmarked green apples, and parried Jeewan's questions about the orchard's operations with unlikely details of pestilential apple worms. There was not much more to do except get back in the car and return to Nainital.

I felt an absurd obligation to be learned, and told Jayesh about Fourier's views on middlemen, and the differences in the price of apples from Rouen to Paris in 1798. I expanded upon the subject with some utterly specious remarks about Newton's apple, Fourier's apples and Dan Singh's apples, but sensed that my audience was not with me and shut up.

Jayesh wanted us to halt at Bhimtal, where, he told us, he had often gone fishing as a schoolboy. It was, after all, his car, so I had no option but to agree.

He insisted upon recounting tiresome scatological stories about the unlikely geophysical origins of the little island in the centre of the lake. I had heard them before. They brought not a smile to Irra's face.

In fact she had barely spoken throughout the excursion.

It was only at Bhimtal, where Jayesh insisted that we partake of over-fried fish, that she asked me in a reproving voice what I had decided to do with the orchard.

What could I say? There was nothing I could do with it, it was a worthless property, unsalable under the terms of the will, useless without sufficient money to maintain it. I had intended to look up the taxation laws on trusts and charities, and to perhaps interest some ex-students of Hiranand Headmaster to fund a charitable clinic. So I said nothing, and she looked anxious and censorious.

Something in her worried child's face must have touched Jayesh. He walked to the veranda of the dhaba, where rows of tin flowerpots were lined near the steps, and plucked two fuchsias for her.

'Wear these for me, Irra, like earrings, in your ears,' he said to her, 'my sister used to do that when she was little.' Even Irra could not resist his charm. She dimpled deliciously, and a smile broke out across her face like the promise of sunshine. Her eyes were no longer wary and watchful. I realized she might grow into a very beautiful woman if only she were allowed to.

The driver switched on the radio as we returned to Nainital. It was getting dark outside, and the car lights swam a yellow path across the fog. Film music crackled in the crowded car.

I could smell petrol fumes and the residue of Jayesh's cloying aftershave. Nainital seemed stifling and claustrophobic. I could suddenly see the charms of a cottage near Bhowali.

THE TERRITORIAL IMPERATIVE

The very next day a flustered Pooran Paper came to Relax Inn to see me. Parvati had been discharged from the mental institution at Ranchi, he said. She was in Nainital now, staying with her cousin Pushpendra. Furthermore, she was intent upon proceeding in court to contest Hiranand Headmaster's will. A power of attorney had already been conferred upon Pushpendra to conduct the litigation on her behalf.

'But surely she is not of sound mind?' I asked indignantly. 'No court would even give it a hearing!'

Pooran Paper nodded sympathetically, a look of solemn import upon his face. He looked so sad, it was almost as though it was he who was being dragged into court over this absurd business.

'All admissions and discharges from the asylum are governed by the Lunacy Act of 1912,' he said. 'In the asylum, they have no legal rights. She cannot own property, she cannot even operate a bank account. But now this Pushpendra has managed to obtain a certificate of fitness for her.' He seemed surprisingly well informed about the subject.

Pooran suggested that I go with him to Pushpendra's house so that we could discuss the matter directly with Parvati. The prospect disconcerted me. I wasn't sure I could handle this at all.

I was by now so used to thinking of Parvati as a motif that it came as something of a shock to realize that she was still around, and in not a very pleasant way. My mouth felt dry and there was a constriction in my throat. I was not at all prepared to cope with Parvati in the flesh. She was a memory, an emotion. She was entangled in the idyll of my youth. I felt that she had no business to intrude upon my middle age now.

I told Pooran that I would defer the visit until the next morning, and sped him out of my room so that I could be alone with my thoughts for a while. This unpleasant and unnecessary complication would have to be dealt with firmly, and I foresaw a tiresome time ahead.

I moped in the room all evening, and told Ram Singh to bring my dinner there. The electricity failed, but I was getting accustomed to this. I ate by the dim glow of the kerosene lamp on the dressing table. I had drunk a lot of whisky, much more than I usually do. The room seemed full of shadows. I spilled a glass of water over the food, and could eat no more. I was inordinately nervous, dreading at every moment a knock on the door and Parvati's arrival.

I fell asleep early with all that whisky, but awoke at midnight, when all the lights came on again, for I had forgotten to switch them off. The kerosene lamp was flickering in its last breaths. I lowered the wick and extinguished it.

I was very restless, and sat by the window for a long

time, looking out at the starlit garden and the dancing fireflies.

Someone switched on a light in the veranda. An oblong swatch of pale yellow fell on the pebbled garden. I could hear the sounds of strange languages. Someone was listening to the radio. I went downstairs to investigate.

Jeewan Jaundice was reclining on a chair, fiddling with the aerial of a powerful transistor. I flopped down beside him.

'I love listening to the radio,' he said unnecessarily. The carcasses of moths spattered the bamboo lampshade. The radio made strange humming sounds which dissolved into an alien tongue which seemed to be saying something with great urgency. 'Radio Tirana,' he said knowledgeably. We listened for a while, then he fiddled with the knobs, and raised the B.B.C., sounding distant and tired.

I looked at the still mountains around us. It was difficult to believe in the world outside. There was static once more as he tuned off the B.B.C. and searched the frequencies again. A gay Russian voice was talking to us now. Sadly he switched it off and put the news away.

After I returned to my room I still could not sleep. I sat by the window, turning the pages of the *Himalayan Gazetteer*. Atkinson has described the Himalayas as being merely the southern extrusion of the Great Tibetan Plateau, of which the Kuenlan ranges in China form the northern slopes. For some reason the observation discomfited and mortified me.

O TIME, STAY THY FLIGHT!

The next morning, before the nine o'clock siren had sounded, I was already bathed and dressed and on my way to Pushpendra's house. Pushpendra lives in the rear portion of a modern two-storeyed building near the post office in Mallital. I had not visited him before, but a young schoolboy, a truant by all appearances, reluctantly directed me there before abandoning his school bag behind some mulberry bushes.

A dazzlingly beautiful girl stood at the doorway to greet me. Pahari girls bloom but briefly, but in the period of this short flowering they are often perfection personified.

'You must be Mukul daju,' she said, in fluent, unmistakable convent English. 'Push always praises you so much!'

'Push' could be no other than Pushpendra, and if so then this must be his wife Abha, the Bisht girl he had married against every consideration of caste. I found myself envying him.

'Push has gone out for a while,' she said gaily, 'but his

mad sis is here if you want to meet her.' So saying, she bit her tongue as though in self-reproach, and gave me a look of such sly and mischievous conspiracy that I found myself sheepishly contorting my face in response. I was hopelessly infatuated.

She darted in, leaving me alone in the sitting room. The walls were covered with several inexpert landscapes, featuring either the lake or the snow-clad Himalayas. They were all hung at improbable heights and angles. I examined them politely. The thickly applied oil paint was caked and cracking. They were signed with bold flourishes upon the left-hand corners. The beauteous Abha evidently also had artistic proclivities.

Abha reappeared at the front door, causing me to start. 'Come on, men, she is waiting inside,' she said, dimpling prettily and suppressing a girlish giggle.

She led me through a maze of rooms into a tiny boxroom, the walls of which were painted a violent blue. One portion of the room contained three vault-like steel cupboards. Folded quilts and blankets were piled over trunks and suitcases. The bed was huddled against the wall, where a boarded-up window made a small alcove. This contained a mirror, a comb and a bottle of Brahmi Amla hair oil.

She lay with her back to me, half-reclining under a quilt, brooding at the shut curtainless window, the glass of which had been painted the same harsh shade of blue.

I sensed that she had heard me enter, but she continued to stare stubbornly in the direction of the window.

The room was dark and musty, and smelt inexplicably of cloves. I had difficulty in inhaling normally. A clock was ticking arhythmically, following and echoing my own uneasy breathing. I walked awkwardly to her bedside and smiled at the back of her head. Her hair was peppered with grey, and braided into an unkempt plait.

I felt unreal, as though I were acting the part of a doctor in a school play. Abha was my sole audience, but she had withdrawn from the room.

There was no chair in sight, so I sat down on the bed beside her. Still she did not acknowledge my presence. I shook her lightly by the shoulder. She bristled and I withdrew my hand.

I looked at my hands; the manicured nails, the thin band on my little finger, the hairs on my wrist turning white, the golden strap of my watch. They were pampered, preposterously privileged hands.

I began counting the grey hairs upon her head. 'What are you staring at?' she asked, turning over and focusing an odd smile at me. 'We have nothing to say now.'

We sat in silence for a while.

'The weight was too heavy,' she said at last. 'It choked me. I couldn't breathe. No one would speak to me. They hate me. I have eyes at the back of my head. I can see them. I have cancer.'

'His feet drove me mad,' she continued. 'Nothing he did. Just something about the way they poked out of his legs. They were such stupid feet! He would wear his socks inside the house. They looked like paws.' She shut her eyes tight and shivered as if she had bitten into something sharply sour.

'He knew I hated him. Lalit was afraid of me. He got me locked up. You see, he knew.'

Her eyes were darting this way and that. She wore a

strange inward smile, as though contemplating a hilarious private joke.

'And then one day he died. Just like that. You see, he knew. When he lay dead his feet stuck out in the same old way. When I saw his body I laughed. I laughed and I laughed. He was dead before he was dead so why shouldn't I laugh when he died? I had died before him anyway. His sister used to talk about me. After he died I saw her spit into the tea she made for me.'

Parvati was no longer lying down, but slouched strangely by the side of the bed. She was dribbling with excitement. Her skin glowed with an unnatural ruddiness, yet her body looked limp and tired.

'I decided to behave like them. I began to comb my hair and I locked up the eyes behind my head. I wanted to send Irra to the convent so I got a job there. I taught the girls Hindi. But the sports teacher was a witch. She pinched me once. I slapped her. I spit on them!'

She spat at me with deadly accuracy. Her spittle was foamy and white. I was too mesmerized to even wipe it off.

'Then one day I was cutting bhindi in the kitchen. It was crawling with little green worms. The more I chopped, the more the worms crawled out. Ladies fingers. There were insects in my mind. They were crawling out.

'One day I was eating a cucumber. Suddenly I looked at it. It was full of wavy little worms. I have cancer. Cancer causes cancer. I know the cure for cancer.'

Her laughter rose and fell. It was like a pig squealing. She turned to the shut blue window and cupped her face in her hands.

'You learn a lot in the madhouse,' she said. 'You certainly learn a lot. Perhaps we could save the legal fees.'

She turned to me again. 'Now you can go,' she said decisively. 'Give me the property and go.'

I left the room, blinking as I encountered the daylight.

Abha was sitting outside. She smiled at me brightly. 'Push will be back any minute now,' she said. She was knitting what appeared to be a blue baby's bonnet.

A young boy who could not be more than eight years old entered the room, staggering under the weight of an enormous tray. Abha directed him with a stern movement of her head to place it on the table before me. The tray was loaded with pastries and jalebis and assorted sweetmeats. A dozen golden apples were piled high in a bowl. The servant boy re-entered with a second trayload of eats. Abha motioned him away with her eyes.

'I do wish for Push's sake that this Parvati wouldn't come here to trouble us,' she sighed, with a little shake of her head. The shell-shaped earrings on her pretty ears were identical to the ones Parvati had used to wear.

'Push has so much work at court,' she continued. 'Do have some bal mithai, please, Mukul daju. A client brought it from Almora.' At this moment, Parvati walked in defiantly, as though expecting to be restrained. She looked at me uncertainly, then sat down on the chair farthest from Abha.

The servant boy returned with yet another tray, this time containing two cups of tea. He asked in Pahari how much sugar I would like, then passed the second cup to Abha. Abha ignored Parvati altogether, and made charming conversation to me about life in Nainital.

'I want some tea,' Parvati announced gruffly. Abha paid

no heed. The little boy brought her some in a stainless steel glass.

'Where is Irra today?' I asked, directing my question to both of them.

'This Thakurain snake charmer threw her out,' Parvati said venomously, stirring the sugar in her tea with intense concentration. 'My daughter has nothing to give. She threw me out as well, but greed always overcomes greed.'

Abha maintained a lofty silence. I smiled embarrassedly at her. Parvati continued to stir her tea. The spoon clanked against the metal glass.

'Irra is still staying with Pooran,' Abha said confidingly. 'After all, she feels settled there. She is old enough to decide for herself.'

Parvati had attacked the jalebis, and was wolfing them down ravenously. She looked as though she were not accustomed to food.

I stood up to take my leave. 'Pushpendra hasn't returned yet,' I said to Abha. 'I think I will come again another time.'

I turned to Parvati. She was sitting with her hands spread out, palms forward. She was examining the lines in her hand with exaggerated interest.

'An inquisitor's hands,' she said suddenly, and gave me a look which by itself was rather grotesquely coy, a travesty of another face and time.

*

I felt a primal social revulsion. It was a mistake. She was an impostor. I suspected her of sanity. I had never loved her.

INCOGNITO

I am in Pasang Rampa's room. It is late at night. My body searches for something or someone my soul dimly remembers. The woman beside me is lying naked, her eyes fixed on the ceiling. She is slender and vulnerable. Her breasts are taut and firm and pointing upwards to the rafters with the calm confidence of twin roes in a forest full of ferns. The night is a jungle; my sexuality is a jungle. I am lost in the dark, I suspect that she is crying but when she moves over to kiss me her lips are curved in a timid smile.

Our bodies meet tentatively, they interrogate each other. Then, reassured by some signals only the soul can read, they are spurred into motion, and we ride each other, faster, faster, our minds hungering, our bodies lusting. It is cold in her room but I am sweating, I smell like an animal. And she? She smells of fear and cheap talcum powder, and suddenly my erection is gone and I am sad and sick and sorry.

My ineptness seems to move her, and she ministers to my body with the most tender motions, and we are flailing again, searching, searching. And we are reaching somewhere, this is a place where I have been before, everything is heightened, my senses are exploding, my skin is no longer able to contain me, my bones no longer constrain me. Stars are exploding before my eyes, entire galaxies, and a celestial music streams into the room, no it is not the radio next door, though that is playing too, a sad Hindi film melody, and now my heart freezes over, for there is a knock on the door, a loud one, and a man's voice asking to be let in.

It is in the next room, I can hear the door being opened, and more talk, and of course it occurs to me that they can hear us too. But we are silent as shadows, we make no sounds as we glide in and out of each other, and her face is like a mask, exalted and resolute. Somebody in the room begins to moan, it has to be one of us. I watch amazed as my whole life flashes before me. I am dying, I do not exist, I have left myself to enter her. And it is over.

I light a cigarette in the dark. I am breathing heavily, and my hands are shaking. I feel as though I have been incarcerated in a dark cavern, I crave light and air. My body is satiated. And my spirit? It is shamed. Pasang Rampa reaches out quietly, she wants to touch me again. She strokes my brow, and I recoil. I want to leave, but I am trapped by pity and politeness. I never want to see her again. Her nakedness fills me with horror, and to the smell of fear and cheap talcum powder, to the smell of magnolias, there is now compounded the smell of flesh and rotting fish and raw life.

There is a knock on the door. We do not answer. She is putting on her clothes. The man knocks again. (It must be a man, at this time of the night.) I watch her put on her clothes.

Her movements are petite and practised. I am weary, unutterably weary. I am still naked, I am cold, and the rough blanket is hurting my skin. I long for a warm bath. I long for Adeleine.

I leave some money under her pillow, then start dressing. Underwear, shirt, trousers, socks, shoes: it is an absurd process. She looks at me sadly as I leave: all women weave tiny tendrils of hope and dependence around their victims. I creep out cautiously. Outside, the night air is sweet and soft and scented. A balmy breeze is blowing from the lake.

I light another cigarette, and a surge of strength and ease flows through me. I am whistling an old filmi tune, and there is a bounce to my step. Truly, the body is an abomination. Of course, none of this ever happened.

MOMENTO MORI

The next day I rushed to Wee Nooke to seek Pooran
Paper's advice.

Irra was sitting alone, doing her algebra homework.
Pooran walked in a few minutes after my arrival,
accompanied by another man. The stranger appeared to be
about my age, and stared at me as though in recognition. I
stared back at him. He took off his hair and bowed
theatrically, exposing a naked glistening cranium. He was
completely bald, and waving a toupee as a magician waves
a scarf.

'It's me, Basant!' he exclaimed, 'I had curly hair when
you knew me.'

I recognized him then. Basant had been far and away the
cleverest boy in our class.

But I had no time for Basant or his histrionics. The
unnecessary confusions with which Hiranand Headmaster
had complicated the tail end of his insignificant life were
beginning to irritate me. Parvati could have the house, and
so could Pooran and Pushpendra or whoever else wanted it.

I would return to Delhi tomorrow, and thence to Hong Kong, and bugger all of them and their decaying township.

I noticed that my voice had become shrill, and that I was talking very loudly. Irra looked up warily from her algebra.

Pooran Paper was very comforting. 'I understand, I understand,' he murmured. He had lit and extinguished several cigarettes.

Lachhua brought in tea and jalebis. I ate them, although I was already full, and the jalebis were so sweet that they made me sick. Pooran's wife persuaded me to stay on for lunch, which they ate by twelve. As I had just had the tea and the jalebis, lunch left me even more indisposed.

I was desperately lonely for Hong Kong, and the smells of Chinese laundry, and the Panthe Kaukswe Adeleine had taught our amah to cook, and my wife's undemanding cynicism.

After lunch, Irra asked me to come to her room. Pooran looked enquiringly at his wife.

'Oh, let her be, she must be wanting to get something off her chest,' Neera said calmly, adjusting her bra straps with a contorted movement.

Irra led me into the bedroom which she had shared with Hiranand Headmaster. His empty bed lay reprovingly in its corner. The mattress had been rolled up. A low side-table held an equipoise lamp.

'I have kept something for you,' Irra said confidingly. I was too weary to respond. She walked solemnly to the side-table and extracted three cardboard boxes and set them before me.

The first cardboard box contained a bunch of letters bound by a thick black rubber band. They were the letters I had written to Hiranand Headmaster over the years, they represented what must have been his accumulated memories of me.

The second cardboard box contained a pair of gold-rimmed spectacles.

The third box contained a set of grinning dentures.

I am forty-seven years old. I have thought of death as all men do, but at that moment the entire burden of mortality came home to me.

'I thought you might like them,' Irra said triumphantly.

'But didn't he—wear them when he was—taken away?' I asked brokenly.

'No, he wore the other pair,' she replied.

I wanted to run, but Hiranand Headmaster's skeletal grin restrained me. Irra handed the boxes to me and left the room. The sky had darkened with rain clouds as I left. I was carrying the cardboard boxes in one hand and an umbrella in the other. I had been far too embarrassed to ask for a plastic bag for his dentures. Yet it would have been churlish to leave Irra's gifts behind.

The first few raindrops were strangely exhilarating, but soon the rain became a furious downpour. By the time I returned to my room I was drenched. My letters were soaked through as well. The ink had run, and they were quite indecipherable. I dumped all the boxes deep in the almirah. After changing into dry clothes I settled myself in bed and lay there for the remainder of the day.

That night, I got drunk. I sat alone and drank determinedly until I was knocked out. It is a useful trick for survival, but one I have seldom had to take recourse to.

I woke up late at night and crawled to the bathroom, where I was very sick, then somehow made it back to bed and fell into a dreamless sleep. I woke again to violent retching convulsions, and stumbled to the bathroom where I threw up once more. Staggering back to bed, I paused by the open window. The cold night air sobered me. I drank in the beauty of the still night.

I could hear a shuffling in the bushes outside. A wolverine, perhaps, I thought to myself, for I was still a little drunk. Then I heard the click of a torch, and a shaft of electric light fell on the porch. I could see a figure beside the deodar tree in the garden, focusing the weak torchlight this way and that, now on the windows of Relax Inn, now on the pebbled ground. I knew in the sap of my being who it was. A restless wind displaced the clouds, making sudden moody patches of dappled moonlight. I thought I saw her smile.

My heart had stopped beating. I knew it was a dream, it was all a dream, a dream dreamt long ago by somebody else.

Parvati was very still, as though she were deliberating something, and then it seemed as though she had changed her mind. She walked quietly away, the torchlight blinking nervously before her.

It did not even occur to me to follow. Although I fell asleep again, I soon awoke, bathed in sweat, my teeth chattering, convinced in some recess of my mind that the dentures in the almirah were chattering in unison with mine. I switched on the light and washed my face and recited the U.N. charter from memory to calm myself. By then I was no longer sure that what I had seen from the window had not been a dream as well.

Things looked very different in the morning. In spite of the open window the room reeked of vomit, and I had a terrific hangover. I did not dwell overmuch on why she had come at all. My mind had already classed it among unreal things.

THE STERN VOICE OF THE
DAUGHTER OF REASON

When I went down to breakfast the next morning, I found neither boiled egg nor coffee awaiting me. A strange hysterical panic pervaded the dining hall. The three brothers were absent, the servants and bearers conversing in loud tragic whispers. I went out to investigate, and found the dhobi's wife in the veranda, wailing and beating at her chest. I was bewildered, I could not fathom what could possibly have happened. There was a smell of death about the house. Just then Irra came into the hall. She looked preternaturally calm. My heart dropped down a long, black tunnel. Something had happened to Parvati. I couldn't bring myself to ask.

'Mukul daju, will you come with me, please?' she said. I followed her out in a trance.

Abha was waiting in the veranda of her house. She looked furious. Her hair had not been combed, and there was a spot of mucous in the corner of her large black eyes. She was wearing the same gold earrings fashioned like sea shells. Little bubbles of spittle had formed in the corners of her mouth. Her face was ravaged with hatred. It was an ugly sight. I realized that she was shouting at me. I ignored her and walked straight in, past the labyrinth of rooms into the crowded storeroom where Parvati was lying on the bed, her face turned towards the barred windows with the blue-painted glass pane. She was alive.

I turned her towards myself. Parvati had been brutally beaten up. Her face was a welter of bruises. Her left eye was swollen and turning a delicate shade of purple. She stared accusingly at me as though it were I who was responsible for her condition. One arm had been inexpertly bandaged and was held by an improvised sling made of a torn cotton dupatta which could only be Irra's. Outside, I could hear Abha shouting at her husband. Irra was straining to listen.

I asked Irra what had happened.

'I woke up last night,' she said, as though she were giving a deposition, 'to find that Ma was no longer there. I woke Abha kakhi up. We found the front door open. Abha kakhi got very angry, she slapped me. She said any thief could have walked in. I went to look for Ma.'

'What time was it?' I asked.

'Two-fifteen by the municipality clock,' she replied precisely.

'And Pushpendra, where was he?' I continued sternly.

'Pushpendra da was with Abha kakhi,' she replied, and her lips trembled.

'I went to the bazaar,' she continued, 'and then to the police station. The daroga was going to lock her up. He didn't know who she was. A drunk had attacked her, and she hit him with a stone. He's in hospital. She hurt him on the head.'

Just then, Abha burst in. 'You can have your poetess then,' she screamed. I wondered who she was referring to. 'We don't want your house. We don't want you in our house. Please pack up your poetess and her daughter and leave. My father has three houses in Bareilly. Madness is infectious. Madness is evil.' She hurled the words like grenades. Pushpendra stood uneasily by the door.

'Let's go,' I said to Irra. 'Parvati, wear your sandals. Come with me to the hotel. Pack some clothes as well.' Irra seemed already prepared for departure or sudden eviction. She extracted a battered cardboard briefcase from under the bed. Parvati stepped stiffly into her slippers, and waited blankly, like a soldier awaiting a fresh command. Irra led her out. Abha and Pushpendra stood sentinel by the doorway. 'Don't send them back to me,' Abha screamed after us as we left.

On our way back to Relax Inn, Parvati's appearance drew curious stares, and even some jeers and taunts. Both mother and daughter were strangely invulnerable, like captives in a triumphal procession.

Pandemonium still prevailed at the hotel. Nobody paid any attention to our arrival.

I have reached the age when one's own mortality is an uncomfortable but inalienably established reality, a faint but factual presence lurking like a particle of dust in the peripheral vision of one's soft contact lenses. I am forever hearing of yet another friend who has had a coronary. Yet, so relieved was I that nothing worse had happened to Parvati that, asking no questions of anybody, I rushed the two of them into my room.

They sat stiffly on the two chairs like a pair of strangers, patients outside a dentist's room. I went down to order some tea, and bumped into Sohan Selfish at the foot of the stairs. He had been weeping copiously. His face was swollen and pink and somehow radiant with grief. He clamped me tightly by the shoulders. 'I am genuinely sorry for the inconvenience,' he said, barely able to hold back his tears. He seemed completely overcome by excitement.

'What inconvenience?' I enquired, quite at a loss as to what he was talking about.

'But you are too kind,' he replied effusively. 'Please accept my heartfelt apologies.'

Preoccupied though I was with Parvati and Irra, I gathered that some other parallel calamity had struck Relax Inn. Upon further questioning, I discovered that Ram Singh, the bearer who attended my room, had died of asphyxiation the night before. A high temperature, a smoking angeethi, shut windows, no chimneys—a common enough occurrence in our hills.

I listened impatiently. A servant's death. 'I want to order some coffee,' I said, 'and two cups of tea, please.'

Sohan Selfish looked offended, even shocked. 'Of course,' he replied, and for some reason shook my hand before walking away.

Parvati was sitting on my bed when I returned to my room. Her worn black plastic slippers lay neatly on the floor. Her feet were not well cared for, but they had remained small, fair and pretty. They reminded me of the feet of the goddess Lakshmi. I wanted unaccountably to fall at her feet, to kiss them, to be her slave, to die for her. I could picture her sitting in a calendar frame upon a lotus, on a tiger, on a peacock. Her face was battered and blue and bruised, yet a smile played upon her lips, a smile of mysterious interaction with sorrow and acceptance. She was my Durga, my Kali, my Saraswati.

What seized me most was the sight of the faded nail polish on her toenails. The vanity, the hope of that varnish!

Just then, Jeewan Jaundice walked in with the tea. He brought it in himself, wedging the tray unsurely against his protruding middle and kicking the door open at the same time. I remember the scene so well—Irra searching in her battered suitcase for a strip of tablets which she urged on Parvati.

'You know I don't take medicines,' Parvati said sombrely, but Irra insisted. She smiled and cajoled and dangled them like a rattle before a child, and I knew suddenly the meaning, or rather the significance, of something which had eluded me all my life. I saw love, and felt shallow and irresponsible.

Sohan came in next, with the coffee which Jeewan had forgotten. The catharsis of Ram Singh's death had evidently run its short-lived course. He looked heartier and healthier than before, and left all in a bustle.

Jeewan at least was sensitive enough not to ask any questions. He picked up Irra's battered cardboard suitcase.

'I'll get the next room ready, then,' he said casually before leaving. Irra heard him. Her tense frame relaxed imperceptibly, and her mouth loosened in relief, but not into a smile, she could not yet allow herself that.

Perhaps happiness can only be grasped in retrospect. It was only when Sohan Selfish came back into the room, knocking before entering this time, to tell me that there was a long-distance call from Hong Kong, that I realized that I was, had been, happy, and that it was time to go back. The bell had rung, school had begun.

I remember descending the wooden staircase, noting each tear in the worn jute matting, hearing each creak of the complaining steps. Everything was amplified in my senses, I felt as a man must when he goes to the scaffold, or returns from a funeral.

Adeleine's voice sounded very distant. It was a bad line. I could picture her at her secretaire, the Hockney print and the rubber plant beside her. Her tone was flat and commanding.

'Please come back, Mukki,' she said (she never called me Mukul), 'please come back, my daughter has had an accident.' I noticed that she said 'my daughter' and not 'Marie' as she could have, and asked her what had happened to Marie. Marie had got a cramp in the swimming pool, the lifeguard had been away eating a hamburger. There was water in her lungs. 'I want you to come back immediately,' she said again.

Adeleine has a way of saying 'immediately' which has always irritated me. 'Return immediately, my daughter is ill.' Then she asked where the medical insurance papers were, my secretary didn't seem to know.

I went back to my room. Parvati looked at me shrewdly, as though she already knew. I was in a panic. I had no choice. There was nothing I could do.

We ate in the room. Jeewan brought up a tray, and joined us for dinner. We sat balancing the plates on our knees, as though we were at a buffet dinner, except for Irra who set her plate on the dressing table and pulled up a chair before it.

We were all silent, eating voraciously. I had not had any lunch or breakfast. 'My friend Beena, whose house I showed you, has run off to Bombay again to become a film star,' Irra said pointedly. She looked at herself in the mirror while she said it, then stared guardedly at our reflections to watch for my response. Her eyes followed mine in the mirror, and I shifted my gaze. Jeewan fidgeted in his chair.

There was nothing I could say. She would have to be wary and watchful all her life, for I was going to fail her.

Irra had persuaded her mother to take the tranquilizers. Her face was reposeful now. Jeewan led us to the next room but one. It was huge, dank and cavernous, with large, sagging beds. Irra's suitcase was already on a table by the bed.

I went back to my room and brushed my teeth, then stood looking out of the window at the still night outside.

Irra came in without knocking. 'Can I help you pack?' she asked shyly. 'I need to talk to you.' She held a notebook in her hand, like a student at a tutorial.

I was exhausted. She had smelt out my cowardice, she could pre-empt my escape. I decided to play the professor.

'Of course, Irra,' I said heartily. 'You know I'm always there if you have a problem. Tell me, please, what the matter is.' My cheeks were burning in shame, but the orphan in me, the resentful dependent, was determined to bluster his way out of accusation and responsibility. Even the thought that I hadn't been good enough for her mother to marry slithered in. I tried not to acknowledge it, but it knocked at my mind nevertheless.

Irra knew that I was going away. Jeewan had already informed her. 'I have been talking to Jeewan daju,' she said, 'why don't you sort things out before you go?' She was not resentful, she accepted my departure, she understood that I had to go. She was no different from Marie, heartless and young and practical. Inwardly I raged at her youth. She could look to the future. My choices had all been made for me.

'I have been talking to Jeewan daju,' Irra said again. There was a subtle look in her eyes. The bump on her nose reminded me of Lalit. I was glad she was not my daughter.

'I have been talking to Jeewan daju,' she said for the third time, 'and we have decided it all boils down to money. Once they get the house they will send her back to the lunatic asylum. She is quite happy there...' a fierce look lit up her eyes which she tried hard to contain, 'but she could be happier outside.'

'My dear!' I expostulated, I couldn't help myself. 'I am a salaried man, I'll do my best but you have to understand my constraints.' Already I was calculating costs and benefits.

'I have been talking to Jeewan daju,' she continued impervious, 'and we could sell the Bhowali property. The interest could be payable to Pooran daju for her care. I will do my intermediate next year, and then I can give my pre-medical here, or in Allahabad. I want to do medicine, if I can get the marks. Daju was saying, five hundred rupees a month would be adequate.'

I did a quick mental sum. It was approximately forty US dollars.

'But who will look after your mother?' I asked, concerned again, for I had got my reprieve, I could buy my way out, and I would not have to pay for a padded cell. Yet I was older than her, I knew it was not so easy.

'I will,' she replied.

'And who will look after you?' I persisted.

'The money will,' she said simply.

As if on cue, Jeewan Jaundice walked into the room. It saddened me that they had set it up, that I had needed manipulation. I was to send a letter after consulting with my solicitor in Hong Kong. We would forget about Hiranand Headmaster's will. They would sell the Bhowali property. Half the money would go to Pooran Paper, and they would settle with Dan Singh, the chowkidar. Although Pushpendra had obtained a certificate of fitness, Parvati was still a ward of state, without legal status. Jeewan Jaundice said soothingly that he would work it all out, he would talk to the D.M. and ensure that she was protected and that Pushpendra got no share of it. He had even fixed a car for me to go to Delhi tomorrow, and did I need any help with packing?

There was something repugnant in the nature of the settlement, in the manner of my departure. I felt rejected and used. They were treating me like a tourist. I was nearing the end of the story, of my part in the story. I was a passenger in a boat which was nearing the shore, the boatman jostling for space, intent upon arrival, wedging his way through the other boatmen in their empty boats, awaiting custom.

For no apparent reason, perhaps just to cheer me up, Jeewan launched into an irrelevant story concerning his uncle who had worked with the post and telegraph department and had been snowed in for two days in the office. After it had thawed a little, when Jeewan's uncle was walking home, he saw a man wrapped up in a fur blanket and stopped to ask him for a matchbox.

Jeewan paused for a moment, as though to build up the suspense. 'Only it wasn't a man at all, but a bear, a Himalayan bear!' he said mirthfully. The bear did nothing, but the uncle had fainted in fright. Jeewan laughed as he told the story, and Irra laughed too, merriment and relief in her eyes.

Then he told us another story. This one was about Ramu the wolf boy, whom Jeewan had encountered in Lucknow when he had his appendix out as a boy. I wondered what the thread was, and decided it must be abnormality.

We said goodnight, Jeewan promised as he left to wake me up by six. He left me his account number in the Nainital Bank, which he had ready in his pocket on a typed slip. I put it in my pocket and wondered if I could trust him.

Irra lingered on. 'You do realize, Irra,' I told her heavily, 'I consider you and Parvati my personal responsibility. I shall always be there whenever you need me. Just now...' She stared at me guilelessly. 'Just now I have to go away because my wife's daughter is ill.'

I didn't explain the anomaly, she knew everything anyway. Irra left, taking away the notebook she had been clutching all the while.

A wife and children are hostages to fortune. Yet I felt alone.

'A failure in love,' I said to myself, and took pleasure in the phrase. It had been, in every way, a surrogate life.

*

I am a systematic packer. Most of my clothes were unwashed and lying heaped inside the almirah. Now I folded them all, and laid them into my suitcase, sequestering the clean from the unclean with sheets from the *Indian Express*. I kept aside a suit to wear on the journey down, and rechecked my passport and airline ticket.

Ram Singh helped me pack the books into a neat package. I hesitated between a clean and a dirty pair of pyjamas for the night, and decided on the dirty, as this was my last night in Nainital. The room, so friendly until a while ago, now looked forlorn, as though it knew it was to be empty again tomorrow. Cleaned up, it would once again be placid and strange; I knew well the mysteries of hotel rooms.

I brushed my teeth, and debated whether I should pack or leave the tube of squeezed-out toothpaste, and finally decided to take it, for I had another night in Delhi ahead before I arrived home.

It was only after I had positioned my slippers to face the bed so I could step into them first thing next morning, that I remembered the teeth. They sat in the recesses of the cupboard, grinning spitefully, demanding passage.

I thought of leaving them behind, but they were Irra's gift to me. They were in a sense, my sole legacy. I could not repudiate them.

I got out of bed, barefoot, and handled them. I held them in my palm. They were quite harmless, artifice not teeth, nor gums, only enamel and putty. My letters, splattered with rain, were only ink and words. I wrapped the dentures in some newspaper and deposited them into the elastic compartment in my briefcase, next to my pen and passport.

Jeewan Jaundice came to my room. He brought the bill for my stay on a chipped China plate with a pattern of weeping willows on it. I examined the bill carefully, and wondered about reimbursement from the I.R.O.

I was uncertain about the tipping procedures here, and sought Jaundice's advice. The bill already included a ten per cent service charge. Both of us agreed that it was enough.

THE SEVERED HEAD

The next morning a reproachful-looking waiter served me tea at seven. I was bundled into the car which Jeewan had arranged by eight. The three brothers stood on the veranda and waved me goodbye.

It was a foggy, drizzly day. As we were leaving Nainital I told the chauffeur to drive me to the Ghorakhal mandir near Bhowali. I was overcome by a sudden desire to visit the temple before I returned to the plains.

I had not realized that it was Dussehra. The shrines were bedecked with gay rows of red-and-yellow banners. Hundreds of bells hung from trees and ropes and improvised poles.

The weather had cleared. I seated myself upon a parapet in the shade of a young oak tree, and gazed at the panoramic landscape before me. The Bhimtal lake lay spread like a map at my feet, and, a little way beyond, I could see the blue smudge of the Naukuchiya Tal lake. It was said that anyone who could glimpse all nine corners of the Naukuchiya Tal at once would be a ruler, a conqueror of the world. No Pahari ever had.

A few old men were hunched around a charcoal fire where a kettle was bubbling. They were absorbed in discussing a local politician from Pithoragarh. 'His father's grandfather was a Nandhoti, a temple pujari,' one said. 'He has crores of rupees in a Swiss Bank,' said another, 'crores and crores of rupees.'

I was handed a glass of strong sweet tea. Two black dogs came and settled themselves at my feet. One of them was a Bhotiya puppy with speckled eyebrows. He examined me with lazy interest. A young heifer was tethered to a stump near the Kali shrine. It wore a garland of marigolds around its neck. Black pennants were strung austerely upon the surrounding trees. The hoarse chatter of crows mingled with the tinkling of votive bells. The heifer was trembling with nervousness, almost as though it could smell the blood of previous sacrifices in the wet ground before it.

A young priest came forward to untether the animal. He sprinkled water upon the calf with a tulsi sprig and muttered something to it in demotic Sanskrit. A small crowd had assembled to watch.

The animal shuddered as it felt the water upon its skin. A military-looking man in a dhoti stepped forward. He had a large handlebar moustache. He carefully chose a long sword from the several ancient blades that stood in a bin near the sacrificial area.

The heifer was still shuddering from fear and cold. The priest announced that it had accepted its fate, agreed to give up its life to the tutelary spirits. The man in the dhoti advanced towards it, the sword held aloft in his left hand.

I closed my eyes in terror. Yet I could not help but hear

its nervous bellow, and when I looked up the head had been decapitated by a single swift, clean stroke.

The severed head let out another plaintive moan.

The old men looked startled, and some of the youngsters in the crowd giggled nervously. The inert head of the heifer let out another loud bellow. It became clear that it was a silly ventriloquist's trick, and the culprit a Nepali-looking youth who was grinning idiotically at his own joke.

The flesh was being quartered into little pieces and distributed as prasad. The sacrifice was done. No one had been appeased, no one seemed propitiated.

As I got up to leave, the young priest came forward with a tray containing vermilion powder, rice and green young shoots of jowar grass. He applied a tilak upon my forehead with a cool, precise touch, sprinkling some rice upon it in benediction. Then he broke the shoots of green grass and placed them on my hair, and gave me some fruits and flowers in a crumpled newspaper.

I returned to the car. We began the journey down. There was a faint pressure in my ears from the change in altitude.

*

I remembered an afternoon in Allahabad when I had stood in a classroom watching the mellow winter sunlight stream onto thirty-four youthful faces. The blackboard stood behind me. There was chalk in my fingers.

'I, too, was once in Arcadia,' I had said sonorously. There was something soporific about the warm winter sunlight. 'I too was once in Arcadia,' I repeated again, rolling the words for effect.

Just then Hasrat had walked past the corridor outside.